I0578883

Through the Lens

CLICK DUET – BOOK ONE

PERSEPHONE AUTUMN

BETWEEN WORDS PUBLISHING LLC

Through the Lens

Copyright © 2021 by Persephone Autumn

www.persephoneautumn.com

ISBN: 978-1-951477-12-7 (Ebook)

ISBN: 978-1-951477-13-4 (Paperback)

Editor: Ellie McLove | My Brother's Editor

Proofreader: Rosa Sharon | My Brother's Editor

Cover Design: Kat Savage | Savage Hart Book Services

Books by Persephone Autumn

Bay Area Duet Series

Click Duet

Through the Lens

Time Exposure

Inked Duet

Fine Line

Love Buzz

Insomniac Duet

Restless Night

A Love So Bright

Artist Duet

Blank Canvas

Abstract Passion

Devotion Series

Distorted Devotion

Undying Devotion

Beloved Devotion

Darkest Devotion

Standalone Romance Novels

Depths Awakened

Sweet Tooth

Transcendental

Poetry Collections

Ink Veins

Broken Metronome

Slipping From Existence

Standalone Horror Novels

By Dawn (published under P. Autumn)

To every person who's had their heart ripped in two. Who thought they'd never find love again.

Through the lens

Photography term.

Through-the-lens (TTL) metering refers to a feature of cameras whereby the intensity of light reflected from the scene is measured through the lens; as opposed to using a separate metering window or external hand-held light meter.

ONE

CORA

Is this real? This cannot be real.

I ball my fingers into loose fists, rub my eyes, and look ahead once more. Yep, still there. Still strutting around like a peacock fanning its tail feathers. How fortunate are we to bear witness to this monumental event? An event we could all live another day without seeing. An event I pray never repeats itself.

For the love of all that is good in this world, please make it end.

On the compact stage of our favorite bar and grill, a seventy-something grandpa wears an eighties rock band muscle tank top, ripped jeans, and faded black Converse high-tops that have seen better days. He holds the mic to his mouth, tips his head back, and belts out the words to Def Leppard's "Pour Some Sugar on Me." Some might say, *what's the big deal. Let the old man enjoy life.* And I would probably agree.

But singing is not all he is doing. Nope. Karaoke grandpa has added a little "show" to his rendition. Giving the crowd something to remember. For life.

Not ten seconds ago, he picked up his full glass of water, tipped his head back, and poured it down his chest, driving us all down wet T-shirt contest lane. The crowd whistles and eggs him on, and he eats up every cheer given. Flaunts his man chest through the wet tank. But wait, it keeps getting better. Now… Some dumbass walked up to the stage and just handed him a soft-serve ice cream cone. Since when did the bar serve…

What the hell is he…

Oh. My. God!

No he isn't. Please tell me he did not just…

My hands fly up and mask my gaping mouth. My eyes unable to do anything except stare. I shake my head, barely noticeable to anyone not at my table.

How is this happening? How is it I am here right now? This will undoubtedly be scarred into my cerebral cortex for the rest of my life. Marked in my mental scrapbook for years of reference. A tale told to grandchildren to make them laugh at their grandfather.

Not only is grandpa up on the makeshift stage, singing to the world like he is fifty years younger. Not only has he ripped off his wet T-shirt and flashed his elderly man-boobs to the cat-calling natives. Now he has taken his soft-serve vanilla and is smearing it all over his now exposed nipples. But that is not the worst of it. Nope. Not even close. Because he just brought the dripping cone to his lips and is sucking on the dairy confection as if his life depends on it.

Gag!

Somehow, I manage to break my eyes away from the geriatric porn in front of me and glance over at Shelly and Jonas. When I see that both of their expressions are equally as awestruck as mine, all I do is laugh. I have yet to figure out if we are fortunate to have seen this. Or if we are being punished for something. It's a crapshoot.

"Are you two seeing what I'm seeing?" I ask, already knowing the answer. To be honest, I want to hear their interpretation of it all. There is no way I can be the only one thinking this is nutty as hell. Karaoke Grandpa has definitely fallen off his rocker.

"I think I need to go home and bleach my eyes. Some things cannot be unseen. Some things should never *be* seen," Shelly says on a chuckle.

"Mad props to the old-timer. One, such as myself, can only hope I'm that fucking cool when I'm his age," Jonas states, an echo of pride in his voice. I giggle as he sits taller on his stool.

And when he glances my way, his sweet smile lights up his face. The one that makes the dimple on his left cheek pop. The dimple that makes me question why we are only friends. Why does that damn dimple exist? Ugh.

But deep down, I know the answer. Or at least I believe I know the answer.

Jonas and I have been friends for most of my adult life. Close to ten years. He is sexy as hell and has a heart of gold. And I know he would be there for me in a heartbeat if I needed him. But I am not so sure if he is long-term relationship material. He has had girlfriends in the past, but most of his relationships only stick for a month or two. And I want more in life than a couple months of good times.

I wish I could be one of those women. The ones who have a couple months of great sex and move on. Just go with the wind. But I am not engineered that way. Never have been, never will be.

Sometimes, I wonder why his relationships have never made it past the two-month mark. Is there an asshole side to Jonas I don't know about? Or is it the women who are assholes to him? Does the fun fizzle out at two months? Does he get bored with them? As badly as I want to ask him, I can't do that. It is none of my business, unless he wants to divulge. But still, I wonder. Often.

I laugh at Shelly and Jonas, slapping my hand on the table for good measure. "Tonight will not be forgotten anytime soon. I guarantee it."

"Word," Jonas adds.

His knee brushes mine under the table and I suddenly hear my pulse. Heat flushes my skin and dampens my palms. As much as I know I shouldn't be in a relationship with Jonas, I can't ignore the way he causes my heart to beat a little faster. The way my breathing turns a bit ragged. There is something about him. Something I have yet to pin down, but maybe one day I will figure it out. Maybe one day, my heart won't be overruled by my past.

A change of topic is needed, especially since sticky, sweet grandpa has now left the stage after his standing ovation. Bringing the brown bottle with the label peeling at the corners to my lips, I peer over at Shelly and ponder over the neutral things we can discuss. But I don't have to worry for long because she comes to my rescue.

"So, anything new or exciting happening with work?" she prompts.

Definite neutral ground. Bless you, my friend. Bless you.

"Yeah. I wrapped up a project for the parks department the other day. It was awesome to visit all the county parks and shoot pictures. I didn't realize how many parks we have in the area. Anyway, they're publishing a magazine next month and hoping to get people outdoors more."

"And why didn't you ask either of us to tag along while you were taking said photos?" Jonas shoots me with faux guilt. There is that damn dimple again.

Why am I choosing to not date him? The more I am near

him, the more interaction we share, the more I ask this question. If only I had a legitimate answer before getting admitted to a psych ward.

"Next time," I mutter. "My next shoot is on Clearwater Beach, for the most part. It's an advertisement for beach attire—on the beach and off—including accessories. It will be the first time I've worked with Global Beach Magazine, which will be an amazing addition to my resume and portfolio. I'd invite you to watch, but that might be awkward. Not like visiting the park."

Jonas rests his hand over mine for the count of three, two, one. *Breathe, Cora. Breathe.*

"When does that start?" he asks as he lifts his hand and rests it beside mine.

"Next week. The first of April. The shoot is spread out over a week. Some indoors, but most on the beach. A few also taken in Dunedin. I'm excited and freaking out at the same time."

Shelly sets her fruity, pink drink on the table, but twirls the blue drink umbrella. "Why are you freaking out?"

"I have no idea. Every time I think of the shoot, I get this weird twinge in my gut. It's strange. I've never felt this way before a shoot. Maybe it's because my name will be plastered in a national magazine next to some pretty boy's face." I wince and shrug.

Snatching my beer from the table, I chug the rest and

hold my bottle up, signaling to the waitress for another round. She catches my request and nods.

"But I thought you were hot for the pretty boys," Shelly teases.

I bat my eyelashes at her. "Damn! You got me."

And then we are all laughing. Yet another reason why I love hanging with Jonas and Shelly. We can say the stupidest shit and there is no judgment. We love each other for who we are and would never want anything different. That is how friendship should be—unconditional acceptance. Quirks and all.

The waitress drops off another round of drinks and I request an order of tortilla chips with salsa and guacamole. Might as well get comfortable, seeing as karaoke night started with a bang. One can only hope the next act is equally awesome. And by awesome, I mean not another rendition of geriatric porn.

"You guys want to hang tomorrow?" Shelly pipes up. "Maybe we can hit Putt-Putt and go-karts at Celebration Station. I'm feeling the need to speed past some prepubescent punks." She laughs then sips her fresh cocktail.

"I'm in," Jonas answers.

"Definitely," I say. "I'm always up for putting punks in their place."

Just as Shelly is about to screech with excitement, karaoke grandpa's competitor jumps onstage. Let's just say she is trying to up his show and is making a valiant effort.

The unmistakable intro and beat of "Baby Got Back" by Sir Mix-A-Lot pours from the speaker. Every possible body part on her body is jiggling as she attempts to shake her ass.

Maybe I shouldn't have ordered food.

Dear Lord, someone save us from the hell we are being subjected to this evening. Shelly and Jonas simultaneously gape at the stage before turning to stare at me. All of us thinking the exact same thing.

"You guys want to head out?" I ask, praying one of them will relieve us all from this new form of torture.

"It's like you read my mind," Jonas states. "You want to hang somewhere else?"

It was still early in the evening and I had only had a couple drinks. I wasn't quite ready to say good night to my friends. "Yes. You want to go to another bar? Or we could hang at the house. Whichever you prefer."

Shelly pipes up. "Let's go to your place. We can stop and grab drinks on the way. Maybe watch a comedy on Netflix."

"Cool with me," I tell them both.

Bringing my beer to my lips, I swallow the remaining liquid and signal the server. When she steps up to the table, I ask her to pack my appetizer in a takeout box and bring us the check.

One more glance up at granny and I contemplate stopping at the grocery store across the street and raiding the cleaning products aisle. Is it a full moon? A new moon? Whatever celestial event is happening, it has definitely brought out the crazies tonight.

Will my eyes ever be wiped of this night? No. No they won't.

Three beers and two shots in me later, and the three of us are laughing our asses off to *Sausage Party* on Netflix. It is a toss-up between Shelly and me on who is drunker. I would suggest we flip a coin, but I don't think that will work out so well. We may have consumed equal amounts of alcohol, but her tolerance is higher than mine. Sometimes I envy her that. Either way, our inebriation is in full swing and life is good.

My eyes grow heavy and I lean more into Jonas's body with each passing second. The warmth of his skin on my bicep adds a new flush to my skin. Like the sensation of a fresh sunburn. Hot, but not unbearable.

It would be easy. Tipping my head, a little more to the right, I could kiss him. Just like that. And I want to. I really want to. But even in my tipsy/borderline drunken state, I still hesitate. I still resist the urge.

Why do I always keep us in the friend zone? What the hell is wrong with me?

Pressing more weight into his side, I inhale deeply and absorb the scent that is pure Jonas. A strange blend of sunscreen and gasoline and grease. His scent so familiar and somehow appealing. Pleasant and comforting and—

"Cora?" he cuts off my thoughts, my name spoken like a prayer on his lips.

Tipping my head back into the couch pillows, my eyes wobble to his as I half-ass smile. "Jonas?"

The air grows heavy between us. The room quieter than I remember from thirty seconds ago. It is one-hundred-percent possible Shelly fell asleep on the blankets near my feet. But I can't see her face, so there is no way to be certain.

"What are you doing?" His simple question comes out breathy.

My brows pinch together as I study his eyes. "What?"

He leans in closer, his lips inches from mine. "What are you doing?"

Was I doing something? I don't remember anything from a couple minutes ago. Having him this close, though, makes me dizzy. Dizzy with desire. Dizzy for more than his lips a breath away from mine. But I also think the alcohol is working some serious voodoo on my organs right now.

A light sheen of sweat breaks out over my skin as my stomach gurgles. I scoot forward on the couch and take a slow, measured breath. My gut groans at me again and I have a feeling everything is about to head south really quick. Or would it be north?

"I don't feel so good," I tell Jonas.

The back of his hand brushes over my forehead and I catch a blip of relief before he removes it. "Cora, you're kind of pale and clammy." He rises from the couch and extends his hand out to me. "Let me walk you to your bed. I'll grab you a cool cloth."

Slipping my hand into his, he walks me the short distance to my bedroom. As I go to sit on the bed, nausea rolls through my core and I bolt up and run for the bathroom. This will not be pretty.

Thank the angel watching over me for allowing me to make it to the porcelain throne in time. Besides the fact that I am expelling the contents of my stomach, the one takeaway from this moment... Jonas is by my side, rubbing my back and holding my hair. He really is a great guy.

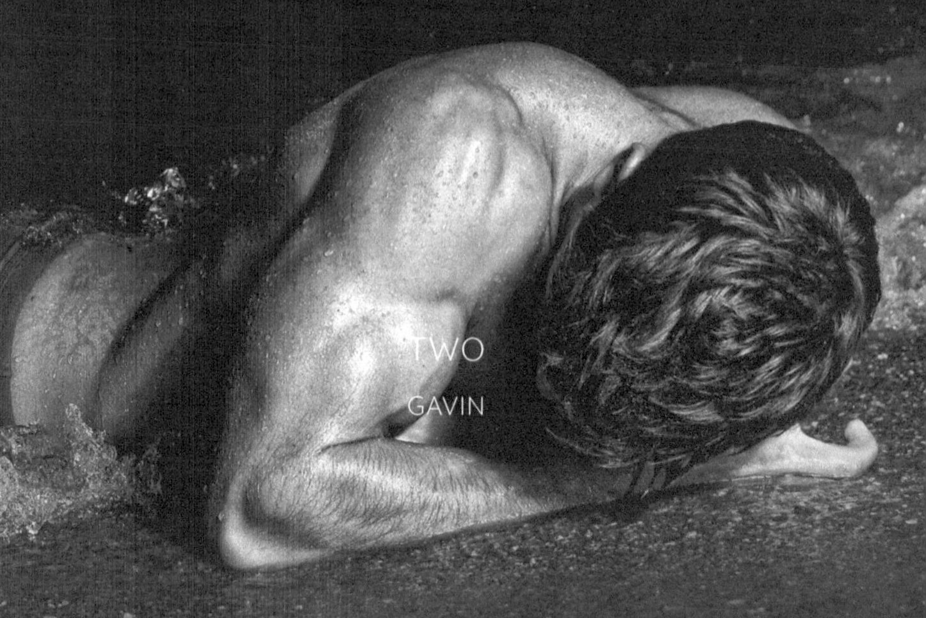

Why can I not walk through this fucking airport without people smacking into me?

Flying is bad enough. Mix that in with LAX during the early morning and my life is a new version of hell. Some woman with a stroller smacks into my arm while the child who should be in said stroller hangs limp at her side. Literally hanging. Under normal circumstances, I might tell the woman her little girl is adorable. But circumstances aren't normal because the little girl is shrieking like a banshee. Limbs thrashing and kicking anything within reach. No doubt the entire terminal hears this girl.

Could the mom not just move out of the way and deal with her kid? Seriously. Why drag your kid around and make a show out of it? If it were my child, I would be embarrassed as hell.

"Gavin? Did you hear what I said?" Alyson asks through the phone pressed to my ear as I am about to knock some twenty-year-old prick out of the way. This whole situation is already shit. Is it everyone-get-in-Gavin's-way day?

"Can you repeat that, Alyson? There're more dicks than normal in the airport today." I speak louder than necessary, hoping the dipshit hears me and gets out of my fucking way. He peers over his shoulder, catches my expression and hustles to get out of my way.

Thank fuck.

"You should be landing in Tampa around six fifteen p.m., eastern time. I emailed the hotel details to you. Please be on your best behavior. My flight leaves in the morning tomorrow, so I'll meet up with you for dinner and we can get caught up on your itinerary."

Of all the things that come along with this crazy job, I am glad it includes Alyson. I never realized how amazing it would be to have a personal assistant/agent. When I first started this gig, I thought it would be as easy as pose, click, done. Good looks should have made it simple. Boy, was I wrong.

Dead wrong.

It has taken years, but I have finally mastered the art of angles and lighting. Knowing which way to face in different lighting. How to dip or lift my chin. How to stand so the right muscles pop for the photo. Nothing is ever as easy as it seems. But with great mentors and years of practice, confidence is on my side.

After checking my luggage, I head to the terminal for my flight. I have about twenty minutes before they allow us to begin boarding. So, while I wait, I decide to hit one of the eateries and grab a quick bite and a drink.

The moment the airline calls for us to board, my palms break out in a cold sweat. I finish off the drink and the coolness calms me a fraction as I head for the gate.

Just breathe, dude.

I have flown enough times in the last eight years to be a pro. Have racked up so many airline miles I can't redeem them quick enough. My job has taken me to some of the most amazing places, within the states and beyond. Not once have I been so nerve-wracked before boarding a plane.

So why now? What is so different about this trip?

The Bay Area is just another sunny oasis with hot chicks and tourists for days. Minus some of the land-scape, it's not all that different from California. I honestly don't know why people prefer one oasis over the other. Guess it depends on if you prefer elevation or not.

I board the plane and locate my seat, throwing my carry-on in the overhead compartment. Staring out the window, my eyes zoom in on the wing of the plane, when the person I will sit beside for the next six hours bumps my elbow. I roll my eyes and shake my head.

Can people just stop knocking into me today? For the love of...

I turn to see who sits beside me and my breath catches a second. A sexy as sin blonde shifts, trying to wrangle her purse strap over her head, which seems to be caught on her necklace. What a perfect setup.

"May I?" I gesture toward her neck, offering to help separate the two.

"Please," she huffs, obviously frustrated and embarrassed with the state of what is happening.

Aiding her with the strand and strap, we free her from the entanglement. She tips her head back against the seat, inhales deeply and takes a moment to calm down. After a sigh, she turns in her seat to better face me.

"Thanks for that. As cute as this purse is, I think I'm going to get rid of it. That wasn't my first rodeo in the tangled department." She shakes her head and laughs.

"Sure thing. Glad I could help," I offer. I extend my hand to her. "I'm Gavin."

"Brandy. Nice to meet you," she says and shakes my hand. "Business or pleasure?"

"Sorry?" The way the word pleasure rolls off her tongue has me thinking of several ways I can give her exactly that. Blonde isn't generally my type, but when it's just for fun, does it really matter?

"Your trip. Is it for business or pleasure?"

Ah, yes. Generic question, generic conversation. I

should be used to having meaningless conversations by now. Not like my job requires me to engage in deep, life-changing chats. Would be a nice change, though. Whatever. At least I get to sit next to someone who isn't painful on the eyes. Could be much worse.

"Business. You?"

"Pleasure. I'm meeting up with my boyfriend and a couple friends in Brandon. I was out here visiting family."

"Cool."

Nothing else comes to mind to say after learning she has a boyfriend. Automatic buzzkill. Sure, I could ask how her visit with her family went, but we don't know each other and it is none of my business. So, I don't dig.

At the mention of friends, I wonder if I will see anyone besides Micah from my teen years while I am on this trip. It will be nice to hang with Micah and catch up. I haven't been back to this part of Florida since my mom received a promotion thirteen years ago. A promotion that had us moving out of the Sunshine state and across the country to the Golden state. A move that changed my life in more ways than one.

Maybe that is what has me so on edge. The possibility.

Brandy retrieves her phone and plugs in her earbuds, essentially talk-blocking me for the entire flight. So much for having a cute blonde to distract me. Generic conversation would have been better than nothing at all. This flight will last longer than the actual flight time.

I retrieve my phone from my back pocket, open up my Spotify app and hit play, looping the playlist. Leaning my head back against the seat, I gaze out the window and let my eyes lose focus on the skyline.

Ten days. I will only be there for ten days. A week and a half. It will fly by.

What is the likelihood I will run into anyone? Run into her? Slim. One in a million.

Majority of my time there will be wrapped up in photo shoots and dinners with Alyson and the photographer. There won't be any time to do anything else. And besides, I am sure everyone has moved away. I mean, who stays in the same place they grew up? As soon as they come of age, most people move away.

But a part of me begs the universe to let me see her again. Even from a distance. See how she is. If she is with someone. Happy. What she looks like. Has she changed from the girl I knew? God, I hope there is no animosity after all these years. After everything, I hope she doesn't hate me.

The plane taxis down the runway and we are off the ground seconds later. I pinch my eyes shut and focus on the music blaring in my ears. The music blankets the roar of the engine just barely, but does nothing to mask the vibration. Or the queasiness in my gut.

Just breathe, dude. The chances are slim.

"WHERE DO you want me to put this?" Erin asks as she holds up the soft umbrella reflector.

I point over to the left of a small side table. "You can set it there. The stand should be ready, if you could put it on there for me."

"You got it, boss," she jokes.

The first day Erin and I worked together, she called me boss. I told her to never dub me with such a title again. Although she has worked as my assistant, we had known each other beforehand. Erin is my friend, who just so happens to help me with my job and I compensate her. We work well together and there is no sense in ruining a good thing.

But since that first day, when our friendship added business partners, she lives to mess with me. To keep our relationship light and fun and not so work-y. So, calling me boss is her work version of sarcasm. And I love all her witty and sarcastic tendencies.

Erin fumbles with setting up the lighting while I do some test shots with my camera. I point the camera off in the distance, catching sight of a few passersby and pressing the shutter release. Pulling the camera away from my eye, I glance down at the LCD screen and view the image. The lighting is sufficient, as is the image. Hopefully, we get all the shots in before the lighting from the windows shifts and adds unnecessary shadows. Not like I can't Photoshop them out, but the less I have to adjust, the better.

As I shoot a few more test shots, the door to the banquet room opens. I continue taking a few more test shots, not looking to see the model or his agent as they shuffle into the room. I don't know much about the shoot. Just that it's a male model and he is an up-and-comer in the fashion industry.

Snap. Shot of the framed art on the wall.

I make a couple adjustments and take the same shot again. Perfect.

Setting the camera down on the table loaded with my equipment, I school my expression and put on my professional face. Just as I prepare to turn and meet my clients, a familiar voice echoes in my ears and I freeze.

A voice I haven't heard since I was sixteen-years-old.

A voice that hasn't changed in the thirteen years since I last heard it.

A voice that tortured me in my dreams for almost a decade.

Sucking in a deep breath, I turn with a huge smile plastered across my face and greet my newest client. *Should I act as if I remember him? Or not?* I am baffled as to how I should respond. I haven't dealt with a similar situation yet.

I extend my hand to the agent first, seeing as she is the reason I work with her client in the first place. "Cora Davies. It's a pleasure to meet you." My smile as tight as a fresh facelift.

"Alyson Jameson." Her overly manicured hand slides into mine, shaking it with no strength. "This is my client, Gavin Hunt."

When Alyson drops her hand from mine, I focus my attention on Gavin, offering my hand. His dark brows pinch together for half a second. Most people wouldn't catch the twitch, but I do. Not only because I am a photographer and part of my job depends on seeing beyond the superficial. But also, because I know Gavin. Intimately. And this shoot just became awkward with a capital A.

He shakes my hand, the rough contours of his skin tingle against my smooth palm. I study him a moment, our hands still connected. Not much has changed since I last saw him. Same height. Same brown-black hair, the style new—buzzed short from the base of his skull to a couple inches above his ear, the remaining hair seven or so inches long and swept to his right. His body, though… time and hard work show as evidence in the taut fabric pressed against his muscular frame. His shoulders seem broader than I remember. And his throat… I swallow just looking at it.

It is difficult to not speak with him like I knew him for years, but I do my best to maintain my businesslike persona. To present myself as the photographer the magazine chose. This is a job. Nothing more.

"Gavin, it's great to see you again. It has been far too long."

Too long didn't even begin to cover it. But no one else in the room needs to know the meaning behind my words. Or the hurt that pairs with them. I pray I have mastered my poker face by now. Because inside, I am seething. And weeping.

All of a sudden, a million questions run a marathon in my head. Except this marathon isn't on city streets, but on an old-school track. Circle after circle after circle. It makes me dizzy and breathless. My heart thumps erratically and beats against my ribcage harder than necessary. Of all the people I would be okay with not seeing again, Gavin ranked in the top three.

"Cora…" he drawls. My name, four simple letters, spills off his lips soft and wickedly. A smile kicks up the corners of his mouth, and it looks like something he flashes with frequency. It is not a personal smile and doesn't touch his eyes. Not the smile I was once overly familiar with. The smile I memorized for more than a year. Those must be reserved or nonexistent. This smile is forced and pretentious and ugly. I don't know this Gavin. Not really sure I want to, either. "Feels like it's been forever. A lifetime. I didn't know you were a photographer."

His words weren't meant to insult me, but they do. They literally feel like a slap to the cheek. *How would he know what I have been up to?* You would have to communicate with someone to know what is happening in their life. Am I right? I am tempted to say exactly that, but I somehow restrain myself. I need this shoot to go off without a hitch. The paycheck would be a great boost to my savings.

"And I didn't know you were a model. So many things have changed for us both, I'm sure." As much as I try to restrain my sarcasm, it pours out of me with ease. When it comes to Gavin, it is difficult to restrain my true feelings. With anyone else, I easily mask my emotions and go about my business. But with him, it just spills out of me. Always has.

The air around us is thick and heavy with our history. A history his agent and my assistant are unfamiliar with. A history I should put on the back burner while I am the photographer and he is the model. This is not the time or place to bring up the past. And if I am lucky, there won't be a time while he is here.

I can be the skilled photographer and focus on the

task at hand. Can silence my emotions. And ignore the flutter circulating in my chest at the sight of him. Ignore the hunger building in my core at the resonance of his voice. Ignore the flashes of our past that float through my mind.

A glowing smirk lifts a corner of his lips, as if he knows he has gotten to me. As if he can read me like he did all those years ago. But he doesn't know me anymore. Doesn't know what I went through after he left. Doesn't know how much I have changed. And two can play his game.

"Mr. Hunt—" I cut the silence. "If you could please move over to the backdrop near the windows."

He cocks an eyebrow in challenge and his smirk deepens. "Sure thing, *Ms.* Davies." His emphasis on the prefix doesn't go unnoticed. Figures he would assume I am still single. Maybe I kept my name for my business. He doesn't know one way or the other. But it is irrelevant, because his assumption is correct. And that pisses me off further.

Prick.

He saunters to where I directed him and turns when his feet land on the fabric. "How do you want me?" he asks with a sultry rasp to his voice.

"Have a seat on the stool. We'll start with some head-shots displaying the clothes and watch."

His smile bumps up a notch and the faint glimpse of his dimples appear. "You know, I always loved it when you bossed me around." This time, when he smiles wider, it touches his eyes. But it reeks of mischief versus genuineness.

If my eyes roll any farther back in my head, I will see the inside sutures of my skull. This is going to be a long week.

Three hours later, after endless banter and flirting from Gavin, I am ready to go home and drink away any thought ever including him. Drink away memories skirting on the edge of my mind. Drink myself into a stupor. Today was only three hours. But there are several days listed for the shoot, plus dinners.

Can I just request a drink from the hotel bar now?

There is no denying Gavin is gorgeous. Even more than the last time I saw him. Time has treated him kindly. Wish I could say the same for myself.

Seeing him today has stirred up so many festering emotions, bringing them to the surface. Pain and hurt I thought no longer existed or held me hostage. But the second I heard his voice; it was as if my prince returned and kissed his sleeping princess. My body stirred back to life and my heart resumed its rhythm. Hope flickered for the briefest moment for the first time in years.

But I shut that shit down. Reminding myself what he had done thirteen years earlier. Reminding myself how I felt after what he did thirteen years ago. And there is no way in hell I plan to relive that anytime soon.

Minutes ago, he and his agent strolled out and left Erin and me to clean up in awkward silence. But not before he managed to make things a little more confusing between us. He doesn't need to say or do much, just his presence put me on edge. Being close to him wasn't always like this. There wasn't always this looming tension hovering over us. But now, how can there not be?

I have this inkling to explain myself to Erin. To share fragments of my past to help her understand my behavior today. The way I acted when he came in the room is out of character for me. On more than one occasion, Erin stared at me with shock in her eyes. I maintained my expert smile and kept my voice as neutral as possible. But the tension could be cut with a knife.

But I keep my cards close. If Erin broaches the subject, I will spill my heart out to her. Until she asks, though, I won't say a word. Until she asks, I will process it all and devise a plan on how to work with him for a week. Gavin is just one of those topics I hate bringing up.

As if she can hear my thoughts.

"So… what was up with all that?" She gestures to the doors, waving her hand aimlessly.

"What do you mean?" I play coy.

She freezes and glares at me as if to say *you're shitting me, right?* Silence stretches between the two of us for minutes—her glaring at me, me ignoring her penetrating gaze. A game of cat and mouse. But the longer we stand here, the more I come to realize she is not caving until I answer. *Damnit.*

"Ugh. Gavin and I knew each other in high school," I mutter.

"And…" She draws out the single syllable and leaves it hanging like bait on a hook. She is relentless and won't give in until I hand her more information. Only I don't know how much information I want to give up. Not that I am scared to share history with my close friends. More like I am scared of what will happen to *me* when I dredge everything up.

"And we dated for years."

There, I have said it. Got it out in the open. The sour taste on my tongue turns bitter.

I haven't discussed anything relating to Gavin in so long, I am not sure if I am being relieved of a burden or gaining a new one. Shelly, and her brother Micah, are the only two people in my current life, other than my parents, who know about me and Gavin. They also know not to mention him around me.

"You know I'm going to need more to go on. Spill," Erin coaxes.

But I am not surrendering everything I have worked so hard to forget in one sitting. I don't mind sharing with her, but will do so at my own pace. And now is definitely not the time.

"Maybe later. Right now, my head is pounding. I just want to gather up all the equipment, shove it in the car, and head home. Perhaps drink enough to pass out, but not so much I will have a hangover tomorrow. Since we'll be in the blinding sun for hours."

Erin nods and collects equipment from around the room, placing it in the appropriate storage crates. A few minutes pass as we break down the set in silence. Just as I think how great it is of her to stop playing twenty questions with me, she speaks up.

"I'll drop the subject for today. But tomorrow..." She pauses for a breath. "You're catching me up on this whole Gavin-Cora history. We can do it at your place or out somewhere. Either way, you're giving it up."

I stop and stare at her, realizing she is more than just an assistant. Erin is a bestie. One I am proud to have at my side. My team. All the years of not sharing this part of me, it was for selfish reasons. All because I didn't want to rehash old wounds. Or cut new ones when hope sparkled in my eyes at remembering him.

Wounds heal, right? Sure, some leave scars. But scars

don't define you; they mend you. Give you thicker skin. Show you different paths.

I am more than that small, worried, heartbroken girl. Now, I am a woman. A woman who takes no shit. Or allows anyone to trample over her heart. And gives no fucks to someone such as Gavin Hunt—a selfish asshole who didn't have the decency to try and keep his word and what we had.

He doesn't know it yet, but because of him… no one can ever knock me down. No one can take my heart captive.

No one. Not even him.

THE LAST FEW hours of the shoot were a blur of confusion. I did my best to focus, but my head was all over the place. Every time Cora held the camera to her eye and peered through the lens, my skin flamed. Yes, she was doing her job, but it felt like so much more.

Thirteen years have passed since I last saw Cora. Thirteen years since I last spoke with her. And somehow, it feels like thirteen years is about to catch up with us in no time.

Just as Alyson and I prepare to leave, I ask Alyson to give me a moment. She checks her watch and nods with slight annoyance. Not sure if it is directed at me personally or the fact I am derailing her schedule. She lives and dies by schedules, but we have nothing planned after the shoot. Sure, she is just tired. It has definitely been a long day.

I walk over to Cora, her hands fidgeting with her equipment. As I step close to her, she stops but doesn't look up. Funny—or cruel—reality, we have always sensed each other's proximity. From the day I met Cora, her energy danced with mine. Her energy is my energy.

"It was good seeing you again," I mutter. For some reason, I feel the need to keep this conversation quiet from the other sets of ears in the room. Alyson knows nothing about Cora, and I don't know if Cora's assistant knows of me.

She sets the camera on the table, takes a breath, then turns to face me. A softness hazes her green eyes. "You, too." Something resides beneath her exterior. Something she doesn't want me to see. And the notion bothers me.

"You want to grab dinner? We can catch up."

Her brow furrows a moment. Eyes twitch before working to right themselves. Lips pinch then loosen. Pain dances over her face for a breath and it stabs me straight in the heart. "Maybe another time. I'm tired and I think I'll just head home for the night."

Her rejection hits me harder than I care to admit. I blink away the sting behind my eyes. "Another time," I mumble, walking away and out of the room with Alyson on my heels.

I am so fucked.

Alyson drones on about today's shoot. Talking to me as if I had never stood in front of a camera before and had millions of photos taken. Telling me which shots she thinks will be the money makers and which I could have improved. I fucking hate it when she talks to me as if I am a goddamn child. How many years have I been doing this now? A decade, or close to it. I may not hold any *Man of the Year* awards, but people know me. People respect me.

When she gets like this, I zone out. Same conversation, new shoot.

While she carries on, we step into the elevator and ride up, away from the banquet room where Cora remains. Alyson gets props for hooking me up at a luxury hotel on Clearwater Beach. This place sits on the water and I have an unobstructed view of the beach and when the sun sets. Sunsets are the ideal end to my day. Hopefully not my life.

The elevator dings and the doors slide open. We step out and walk toward my room. Alyson yammers on beside me, saying how this shoot is somewhat of a new concept for me. How the majority of my work has been modeling for romance novel covers or risqué images. Personally, I enjoy the latter.

Today started a new journey for me. I stepped foot into the world of designer clothing modeling. Modeling clothing isn't foreign to me, but it has never been for an internationally known fashion designer. This contract could take me to the next level. This contract could open up so many future opportunities.

I hold my key card against the door lock and push

through the door a second later. Alyson continues sharing what the company is looking for from the week-long shoot. At this point, I listen to her. This information I need to absorb. We talk back and forth as we sit on the couch in my suite. Strategizing how to maximize this shoot.

Click. Click. I recall the camera shutter sounds from hours ago when we stepped into the banquet room.

I shake my head in an attempt to dissolve the trick-ling memories of earlier and try to focus on what Alyson is saying. But it is no use. An impossibility.

The moment I was within twenty feet of Cora, a hum I haven't felt in years buzzed in my veins. A buzz only one woman created. When I glanced up to locate the source, I was rendered immobile. Confusion trickled through me as my chest tightened. All I kept thinking was *I know that black hair and slender frame.*

"Gavin, are you hearing a word I'm telling you?" Alyson asks as she grabs a bottled water from the mini-fridge.

"Yeah, I'm listening." Lie. I haven't heard a damn word she has said in the last ten minutes.

The second Alyson drones on about the contract, I zone out again.

Cora's forced, tight smile flashes in my head. The way it lit up her face, but wasn't exactly how I remem-bered it. And I never forgot her face. Never. It may not look the same as it did all those years ago—now a touch fuller and more woman than girl—but I would know it anywhere. Know *her* anywhere. Without question.

And her demeanor. Parts of her seemed so artificial now. From the fake smile to the handshake. I expected her to shake Alyson's hand, but mine... I don't know why, but part of me hoped to hug her. Begged to feel her petite frame pressed to mine. But we are here for business, so I suppose hugs would be inappropriate. With my career, I am not one to cross certain lines, but this is Cora. It is different. We are different.

Or so I thought...

But in front of my agent and her assistant, she put on a front that we were old friends, united once again. I know things between us ended in a shitty way, but let's get real. Once upon a time, we were way more than friends. We were... everything.

And suddenly, my wallet rests much heavier in my back pocket, knowing what I have kept under my license all these years. Something not another soul knows about. Something sacred.

Throughout the shoot, I messed with her. A little banter here. A dose of flirting there. Every chance I had to say her name, I swirled it over my tongue and plastered on a smile all women swoon over. At times, it amazes me what I have gotten out of using that smile. But that smile doesn't faze Cora. Not in the slightest.

Seeing as we haven't spoken in more than a decade, I'm sure I know very little about her anymore. Even when I chat with Micah from time to time, he hasn't said much about her.

Micah is one of my closest friends. We have known each other since I was eleven and him thirteen. He also happens to be the older brother of Cora's best friend, Shelly. Not sure how close Micah is with Cora, but seeing as he never spoke about her with me, I assume not close at all. Either that or he makes sure he doesn't broach a subject as sticky as me and Cora.

Even with the time and distance apart, Cora gave me a ration of shit as if we had seen each other days ago. A few times, it was easy to think she was flirting back. Her smirk. The way she peeked around the camera a little longer than typical. The occasional cock of her brow.

She is kind of feisty now. And the thought of provoking her further turns me on.

But each time she schooled her expression, flipping her photographer persona on, all I wanted to do is fuck with her more. And she made it way too easy. Like she was secretly enjoying it. Who knows, maybe she was.

As much as I feared the possibility of seeing her during my time here, feared her reaction and my own, a new burst of excitement courses through me. Every time our eyes met, I put on a snide, panty-dropping smile, and waited for her to direct me. It was better to be a distraction than own how I really felt. Because if I own my true feelings with her eyes on me, she will know.

Without a doubt, she will read every wish and regret I own.

"Mr. Hunt, if you could please move over to the backdrop near the windows."

She was all business. But I was, and am, determined to challenge her.

I used her name like a weapon, shooting it off my tongue in slow motion.

"Earth to Gavin?" Alyson waves in front of my face.

"Huh?" *Shit.* It is blatantly obvious she has caught me ignoring her. Probably didn't miss anything noteworthy. "What did you say?"

She shakes her head at me. "I said you'd better not mess this up with whatever is going on with you and the photographer."

Alyson isn't being a bitch, but the way she said *the photographer* pisses me off. As if she doesn't know or remember her name. Makes me want to grab her shoulders and shake them. Get in her face and hiss Cora's name. But I don't.

"I won't," I promise. And I mean it.

As much fun as it is messing with Cora, I won't jeopardize my contract with the magazine. It has taken me years to get to this point in my career. No way I will ruin it overnight.

But I would be a liar if I said this shoot won't be a challenge. Without a doubt, it will be the most difficult shoot of my career. It will push me to the edge mentally.

Have me second-guessing my every move. Have me wondering if I am being crazy. And I have done some crazy shit.

All the back and forth between us today, I had to have made a dent in her fortress. Chipped at her armor.

"Don't make me babysit you," Alyson threatens. "I don't like being that kind of agent."

"Yeah, yeah." I hold up three fingers. "Scout's honor."

Alyson rises from the couch, smoothing her skirt. "Also, I booked a shoot with you and Layla. It's a week after we fly back to Los Angeles. Okay? I'll leave you alone for the night. Be good." She points a finger at me. "And I'll see you in the morning."

I salute her. "Yes, ma'am."

She shakes her head at me and walks out the door, taking her cloud of tension with her.

As soon as she is gone, I collapse on the couch. This week will be tough, but I don't have a choice. I made a commitment. One I have no intention of backing out on. One that will take me to the next level. Cora is an unexpected surprise, but one I can handle. I just need to apply the techniques taught to us in school. Meditation. Shaking off self-doubt. Being my own cheerleader. Clearing my thoughts of everything not pertaining to the moment.

At times, it can be taxing to separate reality from the portrayal of who you are in an advertisement. Like an actor, I have to be whoever the people want me to be. Look the part. Play the role. Make the men want to mimic me. Make the women want to date me. And with Cora being around, I suspect I will be acting a lot.

And the most straining part of this shoot—not staring at her. *Fuck.* It is incomprehensible how much I have missed her. Beyond wrong to sit there and have absolute silence between us. A lot can be said in silence, but we were not those people years ago.

But isn't that how most shoots go? The only talking occurs when the photographer gives direction or I give feedback. With her, though, it is different. The silence a heavy burden crushing my windpipe.

Click. Click.

The shutter snap will repeat in my sleep tonight. The click sounded so many times today. More than I recall from other shoots. She must have taken enough photos to fill a terabyte of memory. And if honest, I hope she keeps the photos somewhere sacred after I leave.

I wish I had current photos of her. Maybe I will snag one—or a few—before I leave. There has to be a way to sneak in a photo with my phone.

Tomorrow, we will be on the pristine sands of Clearwater Beach. The beach is one of the best parts of this trip. The sand, the sunsets, the salty air. And after everything today, I don't want to be holed up in my hotel room. I need to get out of here. As enticing as the beach is, I need some other form of release.

Reaching for my cell, I type out a new message.

Gavin: Hey bro, want to grab a bite?
Micah: I'm down. Where?

We pick a bar between the beach and his place and agree to meet in an hour. I riffle through my suitcase, toss the designer's pieces in the box they came out of, and head for the shower.

As the hot spray rains between my shoulder blades, I hang my head and wonder how I am going to survive after my time here. Leaving the first time was hard enough. Leaving again will be hell.

My PURSE HITS the floor with a loud thump, startling Luna as she weaves between my legs. "Sorry, pretty girl."

I bend down and run a hand over her soft, black fur and she purrs in return. Scooping both hands under her belly, I lift and flip her belly-side up, doting kisses on her. She is the sweetest cat I have owned, never wanting to leave my side. She also serves as the world's best cuddle buddy.

As I land on the couch with her snuggled in my arms, my phone rings from my abandoned purse. *Ugh.* I just want to unwind and get some sleep before tomorrow. No rest for the weary.

I set Luna down and kiss her head before I snag my phone from my purse. Shelly.

"Hey, girl," I answer.

"You sound beat. Want me to let you go?"

"Long day, and no. What's up?"

"You'll never guess who's in town," she says in a rush. If we were on FaceTime right now, I would see her jumping up and down, hands flailing. That's just Shelly. A big ball of unending enthusiasm.

"Bet I can." I burst her bubble of excitement.

"Wait, wha—?" she stumbles. "How did you know?" She actually sounds bummed to not break the news to me.

I huff into the phone, wishing to escape all things related to Gavin Hunt. But as usual, everything cycles back to him. "Because he's the model I'm currently shooting."

A shriek tears through the line and I hold the phone away from my face until she stops. "Shut the fuck up. Are you serious? How weird. Or maybe not. Is it weird?"

What is she talking about? "Huh?" It is all I can say.

"You know it's not his fault he moved to California years ago. Maybe fate has found a way to bring you back together," she says, words all dreamy.

Although she has been single for some time, Shelly is adamant about the topic of love and fate and how everything happens for a reason. I have lost count of how many times she has told me I will find my Prince Charming one day soon.

While she can't see me, I roll my eyes. Fate. *What a load of bullshit.* If fate existed, things between Gavin and I wouldn't have ended how they did. He would have done more. Would have at least tried.

"I know it wasn't his fault, but he didn't even try for long. It's like he gave up or caved or moved on. Like I no longer mattered. It…" I will not fucking cry. Nope, I refuse to shed another tear over Gavin Hunt. I tip my head back and blink in rapid succession. I inhale deep and continue. "It hurt seeing him today. He acted as if nothing existed between us before. He's not the same Gavin I once knew."

"Yeah, I get that. I'm sorry if him being here is digging up old memories. But you know something?" Shelly's voice escalates in pitch the more she talks.

"What?"

"I love you," she croons, wrapping me in a virtual hug. "And we should go out and grab dinner and a couple drinks. You should be celebrating your new contract. Not worrying over Gavin or the past."

As much as I would love to lay in bed, watch reruns of *Supernatural* and eat leftover Chinese food with Luna at my side, how can I say no to Shelly. Still somewhat early, it would be nice to chat with her about how I am in emotional overload right now. Shelly's the only person who knows everything there is to know about me. She is the one person I can pour my heart out to and she won't judge me.

"I can never say no to you. Where should we go? No

karaoke. I'm still having strange dreams from the last one."

Her laughter pierces the air, one I would recognize in a room full of strangers. "We can hit that Thai and sushi restaurant on Patricia. I've been craving green curry for days."

Now it is my turn to laugh. Not only does my best friend know me well, she also caters to my hankering for Asian food. I also believe I have made her as equally addicted, which warms my heart.

"Sounds good. I'll meet you there in thirty."

"Thirty," she agrees and disconnects the call.

The server sets down a plate of Pad See-Ew with tofu in front of me and I lean over and breathe deep. My mouth waters at the sweet and savory aroma and I can't wait to dive in. What is it about Asian food that makes me so damn happy? No one knows the answer—not even me—and I will die happily oblivious. Years ago, Shelly joked I must have been Asian in a former life. When she suggested it, I shrugged and continued shoveling udon noodles in my mouth.

After the server walks off, I finish my last spring roll

while Shelly begins attacking her rice and chicken with green curry. A moan rips from her throat and I laugh at her lack of shame. It is one of her many qualities that makes me love her. Shelly is just one of those humans who is one-hundred-percent herself. Her candid nature refreshing.

"Good?" I inquire with a layer of sarcasm.

"Mmm. You have no idea," she mumbles around the food in her mouth.

All I can do is shake my head and laugh again. It is at the exact moment when I am shoving my noodle-packed chopsticks between my teeth that Shelly decides to ask me a question. Is that a secret rule at the dinner table? To ask people questions when it is most inconvenient? Seems the case.

"So, what was it like seeing him again?" Her question is innocent, but I almost choke on my noodles when she asks.

What was it like?

Like thirteen years vanished and I saw the first guy I fell in love with standing in front of me. My heart beat behind my rib cage as if I had locked it in a coffin and tossed the key. My heart has never thumped and thrashed so hard, so loud, so uncontrollably in my chest. I broke out in a sweat, nervous to be near him. Nervous to know if he missed me in all the ways I missed him. Nervous to know if he ever thought about me as often as I did—do—him. It was—is—terrifying.

"It was strange," I lull. I want to own my truths, but I don't know what they all are yet. How can I express emotions I don't quite understand right now? How can I express the cacophony of feelings when they're a cyclone in my skull?

Was I ecstatic? Without a doubt. Did I freak out? Definitely. I still am. Did every memory of him come sprinting to the forefront? Most of them. My favorite memories, anyway.

But it has been several years since we have seen or spoken to each other. He may look the same—with the exception of some added muscles and a semi-different hairstyle—but we are poles apart from who we once were. I can't speak for Gavin, but our breakup broke me. The loss of him made me view relationships differently.

Shelly regards me a minute, looking in my eyes and trying to read the deeper meaning I avoid speaking aloud. "No doubt. How many days is he here?"

"Not sure," I tell her. Because it is true. I have no idea how long he will stay. Part of me wants and doesn't want to know when he leaves. "But the shoot ends in seven days. Each shoot is a different location in the area. There's also a rest day scheduled. How long he's here after… I'm not asking."

She shovels a forkful of meat and rice into her mouth, nodding. When she finishes chewing, her eyes meet mine and she has her protective mask on. "Do you need me to hang around more? While you're doing the shoot, that is.

Kind of like reinforcement, in case he's being an ass or you need a minute."

My heart melts at her sentiment. I have no idea what I did to garner such an amazing friend, but I love Shelly hard. No one comes to my rescue as much as she does. She protects my heart as if it were her own. And she knows I would reciprocate in a heartbeat, if need be.

"Nah. I'll be alright. I just need to keep my focus and not let my mind drift to the *what ifs* like it has before." Too often, I have thought over every possible what if. And it does nothing but give me anxiety.

"Fine. But the first time he fucks shit up, I'm kicking his ass."

Her face is dead serious, but all I respond with is a laugh. One that starts in my belly and rises quickly in my throat. The hearty laugh cathartic and exactly what I need after today. There is my Shelly. The best sidekick a friend could ask for.

"I know you will." I reach over the table and pat her shoulder. "I know you will."

PEOPLE. Are. Everywhere. Surrounding and trapping me. Bodies rub against mine. Music blares so loud, hearing will be a challenge in the morning. Micah picked some bar and restaurant on North Indian Rocks Beach. I don't remember the name, nor do I care. All that matters is being out of that hotel.

What I *do* care about is personal space. And these fucking people don't seem to understand the concept. Claustrophobia has never come up as an issue, but in the last couple of days it has consumed me. I just like personal boundaries. And it seems as if everyone has forgotten what they are. Seems as if everyone is in on some massive joke to crowd me.

"You alright, man?" Micah asks when he notices me tense on my stool.

"Just a little crowded in here."

"Sorry about that. You know how it is this time of year. Spring break seems to go on till the end of April. You want to head somewhere else?"

Dragging in a breath, I answer, "No. Crowds tend to freak me out more now. You think I'd be used to crowds with my job and people doing whatever they can to catch my attention. But nope. Still don't want people in my perimeter." I draw an imaginary bubble around my body for emphasis.

Micah slaps me on the back and adds a laugh for good measure. "Some things never change." He pauses to take a swig from his beer. "How've you been, man? It's been a while since I've heard from you."

Guilt rushes through me. It had been close to six months since I last spoke with Micah. Time escaped me as life got busier. But I had known for a few months I was returning to the area. So why hadn't I messaged or called him to let him know? The answer hits me like a bulldozer and I know exactly why I didn't tell him.

Cora.

Although Micah's connection to Cora is weak at best, his sister *is* best friends with her. So, if I had told Micah, he might have shared with his sister without thinking and so on. Things would have been much worse than they were today. And the potential for Cora backing out of the magazine shoot early on was higher. Although neither of us knew we would be working together, she would have put two and two together if Micah started talking.

"Yeah, I apologize. Things have been mad busy with work. Every time I thought to reach out to you, I was in the middle of something. By the time I was free, I'd forgotten. Time got away from me." I give him a sheepish shrug.

"It's all good. Just don't do it again," he teases.

For the next two hours, we sit on stools and drink beers and share chicken wings. We catch up on what has been happening outside our work lives. At all costs, we both do a damn fine job of avoiding the topic of Cora. And although it is still early, we both agree to leave. In the time since we have come in, the bar has gone from packed to overflowing and I am at my whit's end.

Micah offers to drive me back to my hotel, rather than let me wait for an Uber. No doubt they are probably bombarded this time of year on the beach. On the short drive, we discuss getting together another few times before I leave. When he drops me at the hotel, we agree to go out night after tomorrow. And as Micah drives off, I vow to be a better friend to my best friend. Thousands of miles may divide our houses, but calls and texts and airplanes can solve those problems and I need to put in more effort.

The elevator ride is brief. Although I took a shower earlier, the sea of sweaty bodies from the bar has me jumping in the shower again.

The hot water hits my back and I brace my hands on the white tile wall in front of me and hang my head. My breath comes heavy and fast. My mind running overtime as it scans its memory bank for images of Cora. It doesn't take long. Never has. One of my favorites pops up. An image I have plucked from my memory bank numerous times when shit has gotten bad.

Her onyx black hair hugged her face like an embrace. A smile lit up her lips and curved the corners of her pale green eyes. Eyes that stole my breath every time she looked at me. Every time she got serious and told me she loved me. That she would love me forever, no matter what.

That blip in time was the week before my mom received a promotion and was transferred from Florida to California. I had only been given two weeks before my life would become something polar opposite. And like an asshole, I waited until a week before we had to leave to tell Cora. It was selfish of me, but I didn't want to ruin the last bit of time with her. I didn't want to spend our last weeks together like one of us was on our death bed and trying to complete some bucket list.

Does that still hold true? Does she still love me? After the separation—the rift—is it possible there is still a part of her that loves me? Even if the tiniest of slivers, a micro-blip in the cosmos, I will accept whatever she offers.

Does that make me a fool? Desperate? Probably. Fuck if I care.

Her face flashes across the backs of my eyelids like a movie. The way she used to smile at me and press her lips to mine. Heat radiates in my chest and I press a hand against my breastbone, suppressing the ache that slowly builds every time I allow myself to fantasize about her. And after thirteen years, the ache burns fresh.

I remember the first time she laid beneath me, her bare flesh warm and trembling against mine. I had asked her why she was shaking and she had said *because I love you so much.* I clutch my chest harder as the backs of my eyes sting.

We were so many firsts for each other. Relationship. Kiss. Love. Sexual partner. And heartbreak.

And even though I broke her heart, even though I broke every promise I made her, I will kill any man who does the same.

Shoving back the curtains and sliding the balcony door open, I stare out at the beach and notice how quiet it is this time of the morning. The waves break at the shoreline. Salt and a hint of shea butter linger in the air, sticking to my skin. The horizon still somewhat dark with a tinge of peach skirting between the water and sky.

Silent. Peaceful. And the perfect start to my day.

Couples holding hands. Single people with their dog. Majority of the people walking through the sand at this hour are probably residents, enjoying the beach before it is littered with tourists.

I plan to do the same.

Slipping on a pair of board shorts and a plain T-shirt, I step into my flip-flops and head for the beach. The moment my feet hit the sand, I take off my shoes and wiggle the fine grains between my toes. Beaches in California are different than those in Florida. People flock to the beach in California, but not like they do in Florida. Out west, the sand is course and damp. The water cold, even during the hottest part of the year.

But not in West Florida. Here, the sand is fine like fairy dust and as warm as a lasting hug. I rake my toes in the grains before walking to the edge of the surf. Stare at the horizon and soak in the view. *God, I have missed this place.* The warmth and smells and sounds and vibrance.

I walk along the shoreline, lost in my own head for an hour, before heading back to my room and dressing in the beach gear for today's shoot. Basically, I trade one pair of board shorts for another. The same with my shirt and shoes. Stupid, but it pays the bills.

As I walk out of my room, my phone chimes and I check to see a text from Alyson.

Alyson: Good morning. I won't be at the shoot today. Think I caught something on the plane. In bed and not doing so well.
Gavin: Sorry you feel like shit. Need me to get you anything?
Alyson: No. I called room service and they're bringing me the works. Thanks.
Gavin: Okay. Let me know if you need me to get you anything later.
Alyson: All I need is for you to take awesome photos and be on your best behavior.
Gavin: Aren't I always?

Our texts end when she sends me an eye-rolling emoji. She knows me too well. But Alyson also knows I won't ruin this for any of us. Personally, there is no doubt she loves messing with me as much as I do her. Probably the reason we work so well together.

And although Alyson lies in bed sick, an over-stretched smile tightens my cheeks. Knowing I will see Cora in less than ten minutes has my synapsis firing double time. We are scheduled to meet on the beach by the gate for the hotel patrons. If lucky, maybe today I can convince her to have dinner with me. Just me and her. Some good food and conversation. No promises. Just two people with history catching up with each other.

At least that is what I try to convince myself.

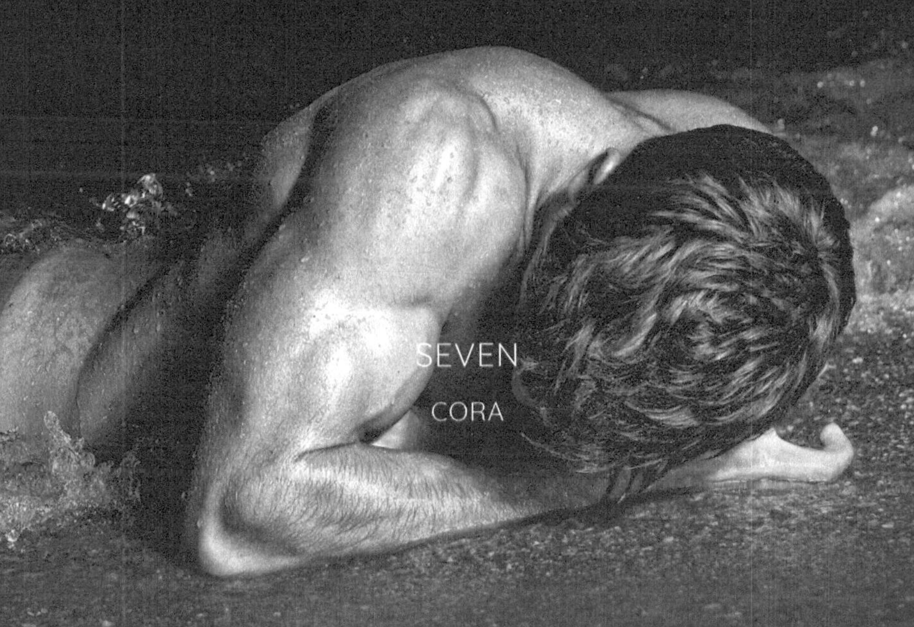

SEVEN

CORA

IT MIGHT BE COMPLETELY out of my way, but I leave my house early and drive to my favorite juice place in Dunedin. When I step inside, the owner is busy making an açai bowl for the only other person. I walk over to the cooler across from the bar top seating and grab my favorite juice from the shelf.

The owner promises she will be with me in a minute and I nod. I sit at the long dining table and look at the cute bohemian décor along the walls and tables. There is a small couch, chairs, and coffee table opposite the dining table. A couple times, I have come in and sat at this very table and done photo edits while enjoying one of their bowls. It can be noisy at times, but it doesn't bother me when I get in the zone.

The woman before me pays and leaves. I head for the register and am surprised when I spot my favorite bowl packed into a container and waiting for me. Setting my juice down, she bags everything and I pay.

"Thanks for remembering," I tell her. Perhaps I visit more than I realize. Guess there are worse addictions to have.

"You're welcome. Have a great one," she says and waves as I go.

I decide to drive along Edgewater and am glad I do. The sun is barely in the sky, so the hues are soft and muted and it makes for a beautiful morning and backdrop to wake up to. For me, to love photography is to love getting lost in everything. Landscape and architecture and strangers. Everything and everyone has its own beauty. My job is to locate that one angle or profile or perfect lighting and accentuate it. The job is equal parts challenging and artistic. Keeps my blood pumping and my mind churning.

I glimpse the skyline as I drive over the Memorial Causeway. If it remains a little cloudy, it will be perfect for taking photos. One less piece of equipment to lug on the beach.

Arriving at the hotel thirty minutes earlier than necessary, I park and take my breakfast to a bench by the sand. I sit and watch the surf, enjoying the quiet before all the bodies fill in the empty sand. I am two bites away from finishing when I see a familiar silhouette walking toward the hotel's guest gate on and off the beach.

Gavin.

For the love of all that is holy in this world. Some divine intervention needs to swoop down and rescue me from this man. As hard as I work to keep him at arm's length, failure takes residence in my veins. Gavin has been—and probably will always be—my one weakness. The boy who captured my heart, held it prisoner, and took it with him when he left.

Last night, for the first time in years, my sleep was shit. My mind cycled through every moment we were together. Remembering the way my skin heated when his fingers painted over my flesh. How he always found a way to touch me, even if it was only him tucking my hair behind my ear. The way his eyes held mine. As if nothing else mattered or ever would. And his smell... an odd mix of beach and pine. Nothing compared to Gavin's hypnotic scent.

All night, memories of him and us flickered through my head like an old black and white movie. And no matter how hard I tried, no matter what I did, the flash-backs wouldn't shut off. Eventually, exhaustion overtook me and I fell asleep. This was four hours ago.

Seeing him now, when he is himself and oblivious to my voyeurism, has my stomach doing somersaults. How much of Gavin is real and how much is for show? Working in an industry where you're in the limelight hardens you. Changes fragments and splinters of who you are. But in the end, how much of Gavin is still inside?

The Gavin I knew, those two perfect years, is not the same as the man walking inside the hotel. Yes, they are spitting images—time has been kind to him—but when it comes to personality… current Gavin is a douchebag. He has got an ego bigger than the state of Florida. And his general attitude could use a little love.

Parts of me want to believe it is forced; all for show. Yes, he was a bit confident when we were together, but he never displayed it in front of others like a badge of honor. Is he like this with his family? The day he acts like a dick in front of his parents is the day lightning strikes me down.

I finish the last of my bowl and toss my container and utensil in the recycling bin. Walking back to the car, I spot Erin pulling in and give her a wave. She parks near me and we start hauling equipment from our cars and into a collapsible buggy. We lock up and start walking to where we told Gavin to meet us.

Erin glances at me from the corner of her eye and her inspection weighs heavy. It is way too early for this. Too early for inquisitions and judgment. *Please don't let this be how my entire day goes.*

"Yes?"

"Nothing." She is quick to respond. "You look a little tired is all."

"Your assessment would be accurate. I had trouble sleeping last night."

If possible, she studies me harder. Her eyes narrow

and her head tilts as she assesses me like a mother. "Any particular reason why?"

And seeing as I am fueled on three hours of sleep and the breakfast I just consumed, I fire off, "Oh, you know. Just another asshole I have to take pictures of." *Damn, I am feisty already.*

She stops walking and gasps, her hand flying over her mouth. "Did you just say that? Or am I hearing things?"

"Depends," I say. "What did you hear?"

She repeats my words and I hear the surprise in her tone. Yeah, today will suck. Challenging enough to be near the man who swore we would be together forever, let alone doing so on zero sleep. And zero sleep means my brain to mouth functionality does its own thing.

Fuck my life.

We approach the gate and spot Gavin. Erin waves his way and I give him a half-hearted smile. The action brief and cold and says *don't fuck with me today*. If he is able to still read me like he used to, I hope he reads me loud and clear. I don't have the time or patience for games or bull-shit today.

He rises from the chair and offers to help us wheel the equipment to the beach. I happily forfeit my cart and follow in his wake as we go through the gate. After a minute of trudging through the sand, reality catches up to me.

"Hey." I tap his shoulder. "Where's your agent? Alyson, right?"

"Alyson," he confirms. "She said she's not feeling good. Thinks she caught a bug on the plane or something. She locked herself in her room and will only open the door for room service."

"That sucks. Is she okay with us still doing the shoot today?" I don't need to step on any toes. Or not follow a specific itinerary she set. In a single day, I learned the type of woman Alyson is—regimented. Organization isn't a bad quality. Just one I don't want to fuck with. Not with this shoot.

He peeks at me over his shoulder, a small, sweet smile touching his lips. A different smile than those he gave me yesterday. A smile that wakes me up further and quickens my pulse. *Fuck.*

"Yeah, it's fine. Most of the time, she stands there and hovers, checking emails and text messages. She feels obligated to be present in case something happens."

In case something happens? What does that mean?

"Like what?" I ask, my curiosity getting the best of me. If I had gotten better sleep, I probably wouldn't have asked. Maybe. Who really knows at this point.

He laughs, his body shaking from the extent of it. "One of her previous clients got a little too *involved* with things during the shoot. So now she's always on set with her clients. Either that or someone within the company."

I am still confused. I should have bought an espresso with my breakfast. "A little too involved?"

His smile glows brighter than the rising sun. "Yes. As in, unprofessional things occurred during the shoot. They were mutual, but it later caused issues."

Light bulb moment. One of her clients slept with a photographer. While they were supposed to be doing the shoot. Woah. Seriously unethical.

"Well, she doesn't have to worry about that with us," I blurt out, mentally slapping the side of my head when I realize I had spoken the words aloud and not in my head. Foot meet mouth.

When I meet his eyes, an odd sadness lingers. I don't think the solemnity shadows him because I said we won't have sex while in the middle of working. No, I assume the actual reason digs deeper. The expansive roots wrapped tightly around one another. I shake off the thought and try to focus on where to take photos.

"Here," I belt out, then apologize for my volume. "Let's work from here."

Gavin nods and walks off for a minute, his hands resting on top of his head, fingers laced together. He walks ten, twenty, thirty feet down the beach before he stops and stares out at the vacant water. His eyes don't avert. His body a sand sculpture. And for a moment, I see the Gavin I knew all those years ago. Without armor or ego. Just the man.

Erin softly touches my shoulder and startles me. "Sorry," she says. "You okay?"

I meet her eyes a second, nod and return to watching Gavin. "I'll be okay." *I hope I will be okay. Please let me be okay.*

"If you need anything at all, say the word. Even if it's a breather."

My eyes fall back on her. Erin is such a great friend and I am beyond lucky to be surrounded by so many wonderful people. I place my hand over hers. "Thanks for always being here for me. I don't say thank you often enough."

She swats the air between us. "Some things don't have to be said, but I appreciate it nonetheless."

After Gavin walks back, we discuss the various images the brand is seeking and the photos we will shoot today. I recognize the moment when Gavin slips into model-mode—the shift in his expression, his body language more exposed, the wall he erects to protect the deeper parts of himself. The way he carries himself in model-mode, it is obvious he is not a model only for the attention or the paycheck. He enjoys the end result as well as what comes along with it.

He may have been a cocky prick yesterday. He may have pressed every button under my skin. But today, Gavin flaunts an unexpected side of himself. One rawer and more appealing. One he should show more frequently when working. A side most photographers would drool over.

Is it because of Alyson's absence? Does she smother this side of him?

We take numerous shots with him in the board shorts, shirt, and flip-flops. We scroll through several of the images, hemming and hawing. After he and I are satisfied with what has been taken, we move to the next feature. Gavin in board shorts only.

Yes, I have seen Gavin naked. Yes, I understand Gavin will not be naked for the shoot. But does that halt the rapid flutter of butterflies beneath my breastbone? Nope, not one bit. Does the idea cause my breath to hitch? One-hundred-percent. Like a damn teenager again.

He kicks the shoes off, flinging them toward the cart. A small laugh erupts from his chest as he catches me ogling him, my eyes averting and coming back faster than a ping-pong ball. In my semi-awake state, there is no point in resisting what I want. Like alcohol, sleepless-ness drops your inhibitions. Makes you do things your rational mind would lecture you on.

Erin giggles under her breath and I give her a *shut up* look. But as I turn to face Gavin again, he peels his shirt overhead with his back to me. As the cotton rises further up his back, I gasp and am certain he can hear it plain as day.

A tattoo inked into the flesh rests between his shoulder blades. Guessing, I would estimate it is six or seven inches wide and a foot tall. My shock isn't over the fact that Gavin has a tattoo. Not by a longshot. Really isn't too surprising, to be honest. What has me sucking in a breath is the art he selected to permanently etch into his skin.

When we were together, one of the things he always picked on me for was my love for *Lord of the Rings*. He would joke with me and tell me I couldn't watch it anymore because I knew every line and scene. I would rebut and tell him he was just jealous and wished he could be as cool as me. A nonstop banterfest over my adoration of the movies.

Now… I stare at the back of his torso, my jaw slack, tongue tasting the salty air. I rub my eyes for good measure, to check if what I am seeing is real. To make sure I'm not still sleeping. I drag my hands away and stare at his back. Yep, still there.

There it rests, in all its glory. A tattoo of the tree of Gondor, seven stars hovering above the limbs, a word in elvish above and below the tree.

As for me, I have no words.

EIGHT

GAVIN

BEFORE I TURN to see her reaction, I hear her gasp. An obvious reaction because she sees my tattoo. But I am also curious if her elvish is as good as it once was. When I peek over my shoulder and see she works to decipher the words, a smirk kicks up my lips. *She doesn't remember. Good.* It will give her something to work on while I am here.

She catches me studying her and stutters. "Wha… are you… y-you had…"

This moment will definitely get stored in my memory bank. Her lack of speech and wide-eyed ogle is absolutely adorable. "Use your words, Cora," I tease as I turn to face her.

"Shut up," she retorts. "Since when do *you* love the *Lord of the Rings* that much?" Her eyes dance obsessively over my skin and I love the fire it stirs inside of me. A flickering flame swelling to an inferno. Will she stare at me longer if I don't answer her immediately?

I shrug. "Someone I know watches it a lot. Guess it kind of stuck with me."

Like you did. I long to say the words, but resist the temptation. Not speaking my mind with her is the hardest challenge I have faced in years. Almost all of my life-challenging moments revolve around Cora. But I won't tell her that. For starters, she probably wouldn't believe me.

Her eyes dance back and forth between mine like she is reading between the lines of my soul, seeking clues to hundreds of unanswered questions. I would love nothing more than to profess my feelings to her. Tell her I never stopped loving her. Share with her the reason I didn't call or write after her last letter. A million words rest on the tip of my tongue, but I won't say them. Not now.

Because now is not the time.

When the timing is right, I will know. And when the time arrives, I will tell her everything. Confess all the fractured pieces of my soul. Spill my heart on the pavement.

As for now, I watch her and wait. Wait for her eyes to unlock from mine. For her to look down my body and absorb me. The temptation is there. Just below the surface. But her actions remain guarded and unsure. She wants to scan me head to toe, but doesn't want me to watch her observation in action.

Too fucking bad, tu es les étoiles de ma lune. We aren't kids anymore. And I enjoy as each second passes and her eyes linger. As they fight against the tide.

We are at a standoff. Pure, undiluted energy spills off her in waves. Anxious and molten and a touch of exasperation. As much as I hate making her this way, frustrating her more than turns me on.

The waves crash along the shore. Children scream in delight, ordering their parents to join them in the water. A dog barks nearby, excited for its owner to play with them.

Meanwhile, clouds pass, dimming and brightening the sky around us. Cora refuses to cave, but she forgets how well I know her. Forgets, regardless of the amount of time we have spent apart, that I can read her body like Braille. I know her tells. Know what each arch and bow and breath and flush means. Know her stubbornness and passion and strength. But I also know her weakness. A commonality we share.

When you are acquainted with another person like I am Cora, you don't forget those little snippets. They are rare gems and get tucked away for safekeeping. She may not be the woman from thirteen years ago, but some traits never vanish. They adjust with the journey.

She tries to disguise it, but I know she sighs. Know she is throwing in the towel.

Her eyes fall to my lips, lingering for a moment. Her tongue sweeps out and brushes across her lower lip. The sight sends a pang to my groin, but I control my actions and don't let her see how it affects me. How it makes me want her more.

When she leaves my lips, her eyes trace my throat in no hurry. Skirting from one shoulder, across my collarbones, and landing on the other. Her eyes drop and her body jerks in shock as a brief smirk pops on my lips.

"Like what you see?" I rasp, my voice thick with the desire my body masks.

Her eyes shoot back to mine as her mouth opens and closes and opens again. "When did you…" She points to my chest, unable to finish the question.

"Get my nipples pierced?" I finish what I assume she was going to ask.

"Yes," she sputters. "When did you do that?"

How cute is it that she flushes a scarlet resembling her cherry lips? How cute is it that she is embarrassed to ask about my nipple piercings? "A few years back."

"Oh. Huh. Well, I'm not sure how to compliment them," she mumbles.

"The same way you compliment anything else." I put on my best impression of her voice. *"Hey, Gavin. Those nipple piercings are hot."* I bite my lip to resist laughing.

She smacks my chest, hard. "Shut up, asshole."

"Ow. I think that's going to leave a mark," I tease.

"Shit! I'm sorry. Damnit. Now we'll have to wait.

Can't have red handprints on your chest in the photos."
She places a finger over her lips. "Although, I could just
Photoshop it out." She shrugs, noncommittal.

"You're the one running the show. If you want to take
handprint photos, then that's what we'll do."

She cocks her head to the side, a curious look about
her. I may be able to still read her, but she has lost that
finesse with me. I have had years to learn how to plaster
on a different face. To pretend to be someone I am not.
That is the thing with actors and models, we are taught
how to be someone else. To be whoever the camera or
customer is supposed to see. We live different lives and
portray different personalities daily.

We are a façade.

"Since the light has shifted, let's move over there."
She points over to a patch of seagrass. "Different light,
different background, different reach."

"You're the boss." In more ways than one.

Time becomes this nonexistent entity when I am near
Cora. Hours pass as if time is a delusion. Tons of pictures
get taken in various places along this stretch of the
beach. As nervous as I originally was for this campaign,

posing for the camera while Cora looks through the lens gives me an ease I haven't felt in a long time. Being in her presence has never felt more right.

Like coming home. *My home.*

I help her and Erin put everything in their carts, hauling Cora's to her car after. Everything gets unloaded into the cars and we wave goodbye to Erin as she drives away. Erin is a sweet girl—timid but a devoted friend to Cora. And for a time today, I forgot she was on the beach with us. Obviously, she assists Cora with her shoots, but most of the time she hangs on the sidelines, quiet.

After she drives out of the lot, I face Cora and my fingers brush against hers. Flickers spark from our minor touch and I feel compelled to touch her again. More. Trace my fingers along her forearm, her bicep, her collarbone. My eyes flit to her throat as she swallows hard. I finish the ascent, her eyes riveted to mine.

Our eyes have a silent standoff. Questions appear as quickly as they disappear.

"Have dinner with me," I state.

Last time I asked, she said no. Now I want it more like a command, but not in a *you must do this* way. More of a *just agree with me* way. I want her to want to say yes.

The motion is subtle, but she shakes her head as she drops her chin and breaks eye contact. "I can't. You know I can't. It goes against the contract we've both signed."

I stare down at my feet and hers, shaking my head. "Bullshit," I mutter.

My irritation isn't directed at her, more the situation. But I bet she takes it as the former. The last thing I am is upset with her. She has to know this. Right?

"You know we can't," she whispers, refusing to look at me.

But I need to see her eyes. Need to know what she is really thinking. Her eyes will tell me all the words her mouth refuses to speak.

Tucking a finger under her chin, I lift and bring her eyes back to mine. She has told me no twice, but her eyes tell another story. They speak of her hesitation and fear. Worried if she says yes that I will hurt her again. And I want to reassure her that will never happen again, but how can I? Words are useless. Especially with our past. Only my actions will supersede my words.

Plus, the evidence is stacked against us.

She lives here. I live thousands of miles across the country. Her life is here. My life is out west.

With reluctance, I lean in close to her ear and whisper, "True, but you don't know how much I want to."

And with that, I step back, drop my hand, and walk back to the hotel. To my empty hotel room. My soundless existence. My life without her.

Sleeplessness has become a plague since Gavin walked through those banquet doors two days ago. When my head hit the pillow last night, my body melted against the sheets as exhaustion radiated in my bones. Luna curled up beside me, her purr fading as she drifted to sleep.

With heavy eyes, my lids closed. Just as my body began hitting solid sleep, my phone wailed on my dresser. I shot up as worry flooded me. My *Do Not Disturb* mode set and only select people could break through the function.

When I answered the phone in a groggy voice, Shelly instantly apologized. She had called on a whim, wanting to hang out but not knowing I had gone to bed early. I asked her why she really called and she told me we could talk about it in the morning.

But I was exhausted and angry and allowed my frustrations to sneak out and snap at her. Two minutes of apology later—and zero information as to why she called—and we agreed to talk tomorrow. Several times, she had done this to me and the conversation consisted of nothing significant. But I was a good friend and I let it slide.

Unfortunate for me, sleep didn't creep up as easily after as it did before her disruption.

I laid in my bed until two-thirty in the morning, thinking about the rough texture of Gavin's hands when they were on me earlier. And the words he whispered to me, I listened to them on a loop in my head, trying to decipher what exactly he was saying.

Were his words genuine? Did he just say those things to get into my pants? Or is it all a load of bullshit?

I felt clueless, and the lack of sleep didn't help the situation. There had to be some hidden meaning behind it. There just had to be. In the wee hours of the morning, I convinced myself Gavin had an ulterior motive.

After hours of watching the ceiling fan spin circles above me, my body relaxed enough and I fell asleep.

My alarm startles me awake at six forty-five and I slap the beast, groaning and cursing the universe. A little more than four hours of sleep won't get me far today. Not after having five and a half the night before.

I cannot live like this. Anyone glancing my way today will surely do a double take—because my resemblance to a zombie will be uncanny—and whisper behind my back. Honestly, I give no fucks.

Luna paws at my face, meowing and purring. "At least one of us gets sleep," I grumble as I run a hand over her soft fur.

She rubs her face along my cheek, silently asking me to get up and give her breakfast. Shoving the comforter to my waist, I huff and scoot up to a sitting position. Luna meows her excitement, jumps off the bed, and trots out of the bedroom. I follow behind her, walking half alert to the kitchen. Thankfully, this part of the morning routine requires no brainpower.

One scoop of food and a few pets later, Luna purrs like a champ while she eats. I wish my morning could be so simple. Wake up whenever, disturb my parental, make them feed me, then go about my day. If only…

I head for the bathroom and jerk back when I see myself in the mirror.

Hot. Fucking. Mess.

A hot shower and a smear of makeup can only do so much. By the looks of it, I need a couple bottles of concealer. Fingers crossed I can perform miracles and mask the dark half-moons under my eyes. *Lord, help me.*

After my shower, I dress and do my makeup, adding more concealer than normal. Not two bottles worth, but enough to feel like I now have three additional layers of skin. I snag my phone from the charger and sift through my notifications while I eat a quick breakfast.

One of the first alerts I see… an email from Alyson Jameson, Gavin's agent. Emails in the middle of a shoot gives me hives. Especially after the comment Gavin made yesterday about one of Alyson's prior clients.

My finger taps on the notification and my email opens. Eyes scanning the email, I read the message twice, making sure I read and decipher it accurately.

Ms. Davies,

I would like to extend a personal thank you for your time. Sorry I missed yesterday's photo shoot due to circumstances I couldn't prevent. Today is a new day.

Tonight, we would like to sit down with you and talk about the remaining days. Please join us for dinner at the Island Way Grill at six thirty p.m.

Cordially,
Alyson Jameson

Why is she calling a dinner meeting to discuss the photo shoot? Seems odd. The itinerary is written and has been reviewed countless times before this week. By myself, the agent, and the company.
Shit.

Did she see me and Gavin last night in the parking lot? Not that there was anything noteworthy. Nothing inappropriate or unprofessional occurred. But that is the only possible reason I can think of as to why she is requesting I meet with them for dinner.

Taking my remaining breakfast to the garbage can, I scrape the last few bites into the bag. At least I had eaten the majority of the food before the taste turned bitter on my tongue. As long as it stays down, everything will be alright.

I do a few last-minute checks in the house before grabbing my purse and heading to my car. My head in a fog, a list of scenarios running rampant in my head as to why we are having a dinner meeting. The distraction gets the best of me and before I realize what is happening, I trip over an uneven paver and fall face-first into the grass. I turn my head and grimace at the paver I have been meaning to fix for months but have ignored.

"Shit," I curse into the wind.

It is my fault, I recognize this. But it doesn't make it hurt less.

What I need to do is focus. Quit worrying over *what if* and pay attention to *what is*. And right now, my sole focus is this photo shoot. Not the man whose picture I take this week. This is my job, my livelihood. The only thing that will remain constant when he leaves again. Because he will leave again.

Thirty minutes later, I wind through the two-lane road inside Sand Key Park. The sun hasn't been up long, which is why the park remains quiet. None of the locals, or spring breakers, have arrived yet. But within an hour or two, this place will be inundated with exposed flesh and sunscreen.

Driving past a few covered shelters, I glimpse the birds and squirrels as they peck at the semi-scraped BBQ grills in hopes they will find a morsel. Half a minute later, the road winds left and I near more shelters, restrooms, and the beach access parking. This park is the perfect mix of park-life and beach-life. And makes an excellent backdrop for any outdoor photo shoot in the area.

I park the car and feed the meter station. Leaving my equipment in the car, I walk down the path leading to the beach and look for potential places to work today. Sitting on a boulder-sized rock, I stare out at the water and get lost for a moment.

Although my job takes me to various locations, I never have the time to stop and enjoy where I am. The beach is great at times—in the early morning or late evening. But I love wandering in the parks and nature preserves. There is something magical about being in the thick of nature. Disconnecting from life and reconnecting with yourself. Forgetting about social media or texts or all the distractions and simply focusing on you.

And in my zoned-out mindset, I recall the occasions when Gavin and I would play-bicker over the beach versus the park. How he stated the beach was superior because of sunsets (on our coast) and sunrises (the east coast). My rebuttal consisted of how the sunlight filtered through the trees and the connection with the earth. We debated over it for hours before deciding it didn't matter.

Spotting a few places, I head back to the car and wait for Erin to arrive. As I take out the last few things I will need, I hear a car and look up. Erin waves at me as she parks in the space beside me.

"Morning," she hollers as she gets out of the car. "Present!"

I am momentarily confused until I see her retrieve and then hand me an oversized iced coconut milk matcha latte and a chocolate croissant from a local bakery.

Swooning at the treats, I kiss her cheek and snatch them from her. "Have I told you how much I love you?" I ask as I bite into the sweet pastry and moan.

Two seconds later, I regret that moan. Because that is the exact moment Gavin walks up behind me, rests his hands on my hips, and scares the shit out of me.

"That's a sound I haven't heard in years," he says then smirks.

Almost dropping my drink, I whip around and glare at him. "JFC, Gavin. You scared the bejesus out of me."

He laughs before asking, "JFC?"

Erin shakes her head and answers his question, noticing how I am hunched over and still trying to catch my breath. "It stands for Jesus fucking Christ. She uses the acronym in public, so she doesn't offend anyone."

"Ah," he lilts. "Still so considerate of everyone else. Good to see the good qualities haven't changed."

Briefly, I want to ask what other qualities he remembers. Or consider good? But I opt not to. The last thing I need after a second night of shitty sleep is a trip down memory lane. Because memory lane when you're not altogether there is a dangerous setup.

Once I locate my voice, I scold him. "Don't do that again! You know how much I don't like people sneaking up on me."

His smile is subtle, falling away as quickly as it appears. His actions were intentional and got the result he was hoping for, that much I read from his smirk. "I can't make any promises, but I'll try." Great, now Gavin plans to use my quirks against me.

I look around the lot, expecting to see Alyson. Although she spends a great deal of time on her phone, she seems the type to be involved. Especially after receiving her email earlier. But she is nowhere in sight. "Where's your agent?"

Gavin gazes out toward the beach, his sunglasses shielding his eyes from mine. "She'll be here soon. After yesterday, she's taking her time waking up today. Says she may have had a twenty-four-hour bug or food poisoning. She's not sure, but doesn't want to run full force this morning."

I let Erin know the three places I want to be sure we shoot today. We take a few minutes to prioritize the order, guaranteeing the best shots with the least amount of beachgoers, and how to use the natural lighting to our advantage in each spot.

When we finish talking strategy, I glance around the lot again and something dawns on me. "Gavin, how did you get here?"

"I walked," he replies flatly. As if it should be obvious. But for all I know, he could have gotten an Uber and let them drop him off at the entrance of the park.

"*Over the bridge?* The walk is long enough, but that incline is ridiculous." Walking the distance probably wasn't too bad. It was maybe three miles. But with the traffic, the tourists, and the bridge incline, I would have fallen over by now. Not to mention the mix of humidity and sweat.

As if he can hear my thoughts, a smile perches on his lips. "I've hiked worse trails in Cali. I didn't even break a sweat. Should give it a try sometime."

Shrugging him off, I face Erin as we toss everything in one cart today. Today's shoot should be easier and less obstructed than yesterday.

As I reach for the cart handle, Gavin does also. Our fingers touch for two breaths, and that old familiar current buzzes up my arms and slithers directly to my chest. Warm and comforting and libidinous. I yank mine away and try not to think about why my body is reacting to his. After everything that happened and how much time has passed, no part of me should be thrilled or eager or accepting. If anything, his touch should garner loss and heartbreak and depression.

He laughs at me, gestures with his other hand in front of him. "Lead the way, boss."

"Shouldn't we wait for Alyson?" I ask. Definitely don't need his agent pissed because we didn't wait for her arrival.

"When we get to wherever, I'll text her. Don't worry about it," Gavin says breezily.

But therein lies the problem… I am worried about it.

Being near Cora intoxicates me. After so many years apart, and seeing her for hours each day since I arrived, it has been a challenge to feign my feelings. If I thought leaving her the first time was difficult, this time will be a hundred times worse. If not more.

But what if it didn't have to be that way? What if we didn't have to go our separate ways after the photo shoot?

Both our careers allow flexibility. And I am sure she travels for work as much as I do. So why couldn't things be different now? Our circumstances are not what they were thirteen years ago. We are no longer children, forced to go where our family takes us. We are adults, and we decide how to run our lives.

So why can we not make this work? Why can we not give *us* another shot?

I want to tell her this. Tell her I would like—after this shoot is over—to try and get back to where we were. Although we are no longer the same people we once were, my feelings for her have never waned. If anything, they have only amplified over time, not revealing themselves until I prepared to board that plane in Los Angeles.

We stand near a jetty of rocks. Cora and Erin mess with cameras and equipment as they prep for the shoot. Knowing they don't need assistance from me, I wander toward the water. Silent and deep in thought.

"You okay?" Cora asks before I step out of earshot.

I peek over my shoulder at her, subtly smile, and nod. "Yeah, I'm good."

After about fifteen feet, I stop and stare out at the Gulf. The water crashes against the rocks and sand in choppy, small waves. Salt absorbs the humidity and dampens my skin. Seaweed and the earthy scent of sand permeate my nose. The rising sun warms my exposed arms and legs. And I am thankful this time of year isn't scorching, but the heat will be here soon enough. That is one thing I don't miss—the heat. Sure, California gets hot, but it's not equivalent to Florida and neither is the humidity.

I get lost in my thoughts, working to clear my head, when flip-flops smack in the sand behind me. But I don't turn toward the sound. Instead, I close my eyes and imagine what it would be like to be here with her without our jobs in the mix. To slip my fingers between hers and walk hand in hand down the beach. To watch the sunset together and talk about everything we have missed about each other. And kiss her lips for the first time in forever. To simply just exist with her at my side.

Absolute perfection.

Warm, delicate fingers brush down my bicep, stopping at my elbow. I stop breathing.

"Gavin," she whispers. "We're ready when you are. Take your time."

I glance over my shoulder at her and give a small smile. "I'll be just a second," I rasp, my voice rattled with emotion. I swallow, aiming to moisten my suddenly dry throat. As much moisture as there is in the air, you would think there is no possible way to be parched.

She nods and I watch as she walks back over to where Erin stands. They talk quietly and I am unable to hear them over the waves hitting the rocks. When I start walking their way, I catch how Cora peeks up at me then looks away. A step later, Erin mimics her. Interesting.

I conclude with this minor detail they're talking about me. And as soon as I reach them, they both fall silent. Yep, they were most definitely gossiping about me. The idea does strange things to me. Twists my stomach in heart-shaped knots. Alters my breathing pattern into an odd staccato. Adds a new layer of sweat beneath my salty, humid skin. Makes my fingers fidget enough that I want to shove them in my pockets. Pockets I don't have today.

Cora's eyes refuse to meet mine. If honest with myself, I would venture to guess she is avoiding eye contact on purpose. But her avoidance isn't cold. It's as if she donned a new suit of armor, the type designed for the sole purpose of protecting one's heart. Her heart. The same heart I shattered into a million shards. And another blade stabs me for what I did to her. What I could have fixed if I had the balls to do it.

My heart beats so violently, as if it's trying to rip its way out of my chest. But the pericardium encasing my heart holds it back, restrains me, as hers does the same. I have to keep reminding myself, I am the reason for her walls. I am the reason she keeps telling me no. But I also hope to be the reason those walls come down.

We are ten minutes into the shoot when Alyson approaches. For someone who said she was on death's door yesterday, she looks a few shades tanner. Maybe it's the white summer apparel she wears, making her skin pop against the stark color. Or maybe she wanted to enjoy a little downtime while here, knowing she could trust me to do the right thing.

No matter. Neither scenario bothers me. Just glad she is okay. Alyson may be the bridezilla version of a talent agent, but I have known her years and still care about her as a person.

We finish up shooting near the rocks, then spend an

hour snapping photos by seagrasses. The shoot wraps after we take numerous photos on a path resembling a pier in the sand. Cora takes photos from several different angles and I honestly cannot wait to see the end results.

Erin packs a few things into the cart when I approach Cora. "So, I'll see you at six-thirty?"

She checks her watch, noting our dinner is a little more than three hours from now. "Yes, I'll be there. I let Alyson know earlier."

Right, Alyson. I ignore the idea of Alyson disrupting dinner and change the topic.

"Do you need help?" I point to the cart.

"No, I'm good. Thanks, though."

We all shuffle back to the cars. And although I walked here this morning, the temperature is much warmer now and I don't want to spend over an hour with the heat beating down on me. I ask Alyson for a ride back. She concedes and we hop in the rental after saying goodbye to Cora and Erin.

We are out of the park and turning off the bridge when Alyson turns down the radio, muting the local rock station. "So, what's the plan for tonight?"

I peer over at her, her eyes glued to the road as she watches for pedestrians. "Not sure I understand the question," I answer. I have an idea of where this is headed, but I won't put words in her mouth or give her fuel for the fire.

Stopped at a red light for Hamden Drive, she faces

me a second and then returns her eyes to the street. "The dinner *meeting*." I don't miss the way she emphasizes the word meeting. Her tone mirroring a bad taste on her tongue. Yep. Just as I suspected.

"I thought we already discussed this. I really don't feel like repeating myself," I clip.

She turns onto Hamden and we wade through traffic for the next twenty minutes. Not another word passes between us and the silence leans more toward uncomfortable than not.

Once she parks the car, we head into the hotel. I press the call button for the elevator and notice her slight fidget as we wait.

Is she nervous? Why the hell would she be nervous?

"You okay?" I ask as the elevator car arrives and we step in.

We press the buttons for our respective floors and the doors close. Once we are in the confines of the elevator, she answers, "I'm fine. Just…"

I hold up a hand, stopping her from continuing. Already aware of what she is going to say. She is warning me. Telling me to *be on my best behavior*. As if I am a fucking child. As if I am her former client who liked to stick his dick in anything with a hole. I understand her role in our business relationship, but she needs to give me some slack. She needs to trust me.

The elevator pings for her floor and she hesitates a

moment. A second later, she steps out and faces me. "Enjoy your dinner, Gavin."

I nod, a snide smile on my face. *Thanks, I will.*

Searching through my memory, I cannot recall a time I remember being as nervous as I am right now. It has been ten minutes since the host seated me. Eight minutes since the server came to the table, pouring two glasses of ice water and asking if I would prefer something else to drink. Five minutes since I picked up the menu, scanned the options but didn't read a single word of it.

But none of that matters. None of it.

As I twist and untwist the cloth napkin in my lap, the only thing that matters is standing at the host podium. She is utter perfection. And I am second-guessing this whole situation I masterminded.

While she waits for the host to return and direct her to the table, I sit in silence and watch her. Her silky, straight hair grazes the tops of her shoulders. The inky black strands parted off-center, the side with less hair tucked behind her ear. The other side hangs straight and blankets half of her cheek.

God, I miss running my fingers through her hair.

She bounces from one leg to the other as she waits, her bare calves accentuated by the black chunky-heeled Mary Jane's she wears. My eyes stroll up the length of her body, pausing and relishing on the dress that stops just above her knees. It hugs her body like a glove. Matching her hair and shoes, it's black in color but embellished with large rivets.

This is my Cora. The girl I knew all those years ago. The girl I fell in love with. The woman I still love.

Regardless of how much time has passed, she still manages to keep the root of who she is alive. And although she dresses as expected for her career, she hasn't abandoned who she is at heart.

The host returns to the podium and they exchange words, her smile lighting up the room before he turns to walk her to the table. Should I keep my eyes on her? Or should I avert my gaze and play it cool? As if I wait for her arrival disinterested.

The napkin rubs against my palms as I wring the cloth tighter. When she sees me—and only me—her brows scrunch in question. She stands ten feet from the table when a bead of sweat rolls down the side of my neck. Five feet when I swallow the boulder in my throat.

I can do this.

"Hey," I stammer as she sits, the host unfolding her napkin and offering to place it in her lap.

Once the host walks away, she looks around the room

before circling back to me. "Hi," she says. "Where's Alyson?"

I don't want to lie to her, but I fear what she will do when I tell her the truth. If I ever want anything more with her again, I can't lie. Honesty is essential. No matter the consequences.

"Not sure. She's doing her own thing. Exploring the area and whatnot."

I mentally prepare for the backlash. The anger. For her to get up and stomp off and not talk to me again. Because she has to be upset at the fact that I coordinated a dinner with her and made her believe it was a meeting.

My eyes dart between hers, watching her expression and waiting for the fire that is bound to blaze at any moment. But I don't see anger. Confusion still paints lines on her forehead, her eyes pinching at the corners.

"So, there's no meeting?"

"Sorry to disappoint," I tell her.

Her shoulders drop as she exhales a deep breath. *Was the idea of having a meeting a concern for her?* I hadn't read the email Alyson sent Cora, but I told her to make certain it was vague. Had it been so vague she was concerned for her job? *Shit.*

"You okay?" I ask.

"Yeah. I've just been pondering over why we were having a meeting. Everything has been laid out since the beginning, so I wasn't sure if something had changed. I'm relieved everything's good." She takes a sip of her water, sets the glass down, and then points her finger at me. "You, on the other hand, I'm a little peeved at."

I knew I wouldn't be let off the hook so easily, but I feign innocence for shiggles. "Me? What did I do?" I press a hand against my chest and pop my mouth open in mock horror.

"Please," she drawls out the word, lacing it with sarcasm and making me smile. "You've asked me to have dinner with you twice. Both times I've told you no. So instead of hearing a third rejection, you tell your *I'll-kiss-your-ass-every-day-of-the-week* agent to orchestrate a phony dinner meeting and not be at said meeting. Am I missing anything?"

Her spunk and tenacity spark a thrill in my chest, a fire I haven't felt in years. If anything, her spunk seems to have grown. I would give up everything to keep our fire burning. To keep her.

"You kept saying no. How else am I supposed to get you to have dinner with me?" I joke.

She rolls her eyes. "I don't know, maybe ask another time or two. I would've caved."

That's an admission I wasn't expecting. *She would have given in? She would have said yes?* This adds a whole new layer to our already complicated situation. I open my mouth to respond, but have absolutely no idea what to say. So, I close my mouth and simply stare at her awestruck.

"Yes. Eventually I would have said yes," she admits.

Wait… what? "Did I just say that out loud?"

"If you mean, *she would have said yes?* Then yes, you said it out loud."

Fuck my head for not operating at full capacity.

"Well, I'm humiliated," I tell her, heat crawling up my neck and scorching my face. I pick up my water and down half the glass.

"Gavin…" she says my name like it's her favorite, and not, at the same time. "I need this contract. This is huge for me." Her words are a plea for understanding. "I can't risk messing it up. This shoot will be the most valuable item on my future resume. When future clients see that I've done a shoot for Global Beach Magazine, it'll push me to the next level. Open doors I've dreamed about for years."

I stare at the empty white plate in front of me, nodding in realization. Me asking her to dinner could royally screw her career. The contract we each signed explicitly stated no fraternization between the model and photographer. And my selfishness could fuck that up for her. "Sorry," I whisper.

She reaches over and places her hand on mine. The heat from her skin penetrates mine, sending a ripple of emotions from my fingertips to my core. I have no idea how I survived the last thirteen years without her. Without her touch, without her embrace, without her lips on mine.

"Don't apologize. I just need you to understand. This

career is my life and I have to be careful not to jeopardize it," Cora states as her forehead scrunches.

"I get it. Things are somewhat the same for me. Sure, I could justify us having dinner together as being old friends, but I know it's more than that. At least it is for me."

Cora opens her mouth to respond, but is cut off when the server sidles up beside the table and asks for our drink orders. We order drinks, telling the server we need a few more minutes before ordering our meals.

The moment he walks away, I catch her watching me. Her green eyes soft and caring. She doesn't say a word. Doesn't have to. We lock eyes for twenty rapid beats of my heart before my eyes break away first.

I am so fucked.

"We should probably decide what we're eating before the server returns," I tell her.

With a nod, she removes her hand from mine and picks up her menu. The heat she ignited minutes ago… it evaporates the second her skin leaves mine.

And now, I will do whatever necessary to have it again.

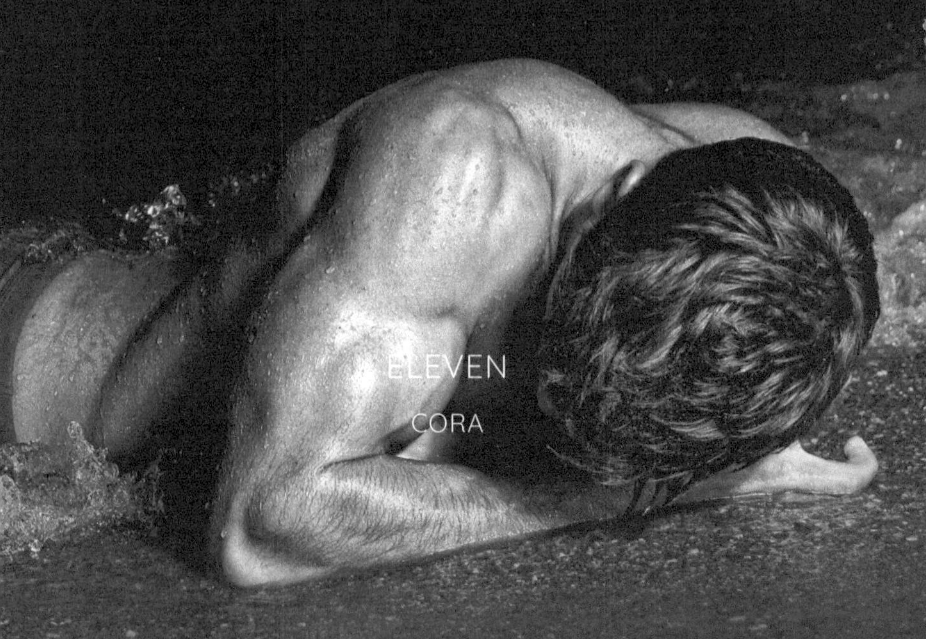

ELEVEN

CORA

AFTER THE SERVER takes our dinner order, Gavin and I fall into comfortable conversation. Although we had once known everything about each other, there is so much we don't know now. We spend the time, before our dinner arrives, playing twenty questions.

I ask him about California. What he likes and dislikes. His favorite places there. Where else he has traveled for work. What he does when he isn't working.

As challenging as it is, I do my best to steer clear of the topic of him leaving. The first time as well as the next time. It's inevitable he will leave again. And as much as I hate the idea of him leaving, I remind myself of this regularly. His home is thousands of miles from here. Everything he has is there—family, career, friends— waiting for him to return.

Another topic I dare not mention... relationship status. His or my own.

The way he has acted around me, I am unsure how to digest it all. Is it just old feelings coming to the surface because he is here again? Does he act like this with other women photographers? Or women of interest in general? Is he a player? Is he playing me?

But the biggest of them all... does he have someone waiting in California for his return?

After all these years, there is no way Gavin is single. It isn't possible. Yes, he is busy with his career. But a busy career doesn't equal single status. Not with his good looks.

My endless mental list of questions is disrupted when the server sets a plate of coconut shrimp and coconut almond rice in front of me. I lean over the plate and inhale the delicious aroma, moaning my delight.

Gavin laughs, "Now that's a sound I haven't heard in a long time. Not quite the same as your breakfast today." He gazes at me with a tenderness I haven't seen in a long time. A tenderness I am all too familiar with. Hummingbirds take flight in my chest, flapping their wings beneath my sternum and causing palpitations.

I play it off and swat him with my napkin. "Shut up," I say with a giggle.

We eat and laugh and share great conversation over dinner. Being here with Gavin feels normal. Natural. When we finish eating, he asks if I will meet him at an ice cream shop across from his hotel. Without hesitation, I tell him yes.

Tonight has been fun. It has been a long time since I have been this relaxed and more myself. As if a part of me has returned with Gavin here. I miss that part of myself. The carefree, jubilant, and eccentric girl. He has been the only person who loved every side of me. And the only person I have exposed so much of myself to.

When he moved away, a slice of me went with him. The piece of me reserved only for him. The piece that feels as if it has returned home.

We stroll down Mandalay Avenue, hands clasped while he eats a cone topped with cookie dough ice cream and mine topped with mint avalanche. Our hands swing between us, our lips silent as we consume our confections.

Simple moments like this are ones I will never forget. Memories stashed away for the days when he is gone. Memories of all the wonderful times we have shared.

We don't need to say anything. We don't have to do anything. As long as it is just us, everything in life is perfect. Our time apart resides in some nether region of the universe.

At a crosswalk, we wait for the traffic to stop and move to the beachside of the street. He leads us down one of the small side streets and toward a public access point for the beach. As he pops the last of his cone in his mouth, he bends and begins removing his shoes.

"Will you walk with me?" he asks as he stands upright. His love for the beach hasn't vanished over the years. He was lucky his mom's promotion led them to another coastal state. If Gavin didn't have the beach, I don't think he would be whole. Not sure if it's the sand or the water or the salty air, but Gavin was born to be near a beach.

Part of me wants to give him a hard time and say *isn't that what we've been doing?* But I stop myself. It's one thing to weave in and out of people on a busy, pedestrian-loaded street. It is completely different to step onto the fine-grained beach, barefoot, and walk in the dark along the surf holding someone's hand. Though the beach may not be pitch black, it's dark enough to make the level of intimacy go from zero to one hundred in seconds.

He studies my face, waiting for me to answer. I take the last bite of my cone, buying myself a few more seconds. I reach forward and take his hand again, squeeze it gently and nod. Before I bend down to remove my shoes, I catch a glimpse of the smile I remember. The smile that flashes in my memories. The smile that lured me in when I was fourteen.

I park in my driveway and grab my purse and shoes from the passenger seat before getting out. My thoughts swim and swirl and blend together. Old memories of Gavin and me. Happy memories. Memories I will never forget.

Once inside, I add food to Luna's bowl and pet her a few times before heading for my bedroom. I toss my shoes in the closet and strip off my dress, heading for the shower. The walk on the beach with Gavin was wonderful, but I need to wash the sticky beach air and sand off my skin.

With a towel wrapped around my torso, I dig through my dresser and grab a pair of boy shorts and a tank top. Clad in my nightwear, I plop down on my bed and flick on the television, scanning Netflix for something to watch. I pick a random movie, which ends up becoming background noise to my racing mind.

A pair of warm hands cover my eyes, too large to belong to any girl I know. His hot breath on my ear sends a chill down my spine. My breath hitches and my heart beats as if it will never have the chance after today.

"Guess who…" his whisper like sun and thunder and a bolt of lightning to my heart.

"Hmm…" I toy with him. "I can't be sure. Jake?" I tease.

His hands rip from my eyes, the bright light instantly

returns and makes me squint. "Who?" He spins me around and hugs me so tight I can't speak.

"Nope, not Jake," I joke again.

"Who the hell is Jake?" he asks, defensive.

I love it when he becomes possessive. "I don't know. Just made up the name to mess with you. Of course I knew it was you." Pushing up onto my tiptoes, I press a kiss on the corner of his mouth. "Don't be mad."

"I'm not mad," he mumbles, but the grumpy doesn't leave his face. We are about to turn the corner in the hallway when he lifts me up and hoists me over his shoulder, fireman-style. Everyone at their lockers starts laughing at the spectacle. And it is most definitely a spectacle.

Because as he is walking down the hall with me over his shoulder, I am smacking his ass and kicking my feet in the air, begging for him to put me down. It wouldn't shock me if this scene floods the internet once it ends.

As we walk out the double doors, his stride grows faster and more urgent. He stops next to a big oak—our tree—and sets me on the ground, smacking my ass for good measure.

"Gavin! Why did you do that? That was so embarrassing." It was beyond embarrassing, yet I loved every second of it. Loved that he didn't care who was watching.

He takes a step closer to me, eliminating the empty space between us. I suck in a breath, my body straightening and my breasts brushing against his chest. His hands dance along my jawline before his fingers lace in my hair and he brings his mouth to mine.

He kisses me with such intensity, I forget how to breathe. His tongue traces over my lower lip and I open for him. Our tongues begin this wild dance, fevered and needy. Wolf whistles erupt around us, but we ignore every one of them. It is just me and Gavin as the world disappears. And as quickly as the kiss began, it ends.

I grab hold of his biceps, dragging in ragged breaths while trying to calm my heart.

"You are forgiven," I tell him when my lungs settle.

He presses a sweet kiss to the center of my lips. "Thanks."

When he pulls away from our embrace, he looks over at the tree beside us. My eyes shift to see what he is looking at, and my jaw falls to the ground.

"When? How? Did you?" I fumble over what I am trying to ask him.

"This morning. With the pocket knife I snuck into school. And yes, I did."

My fingers brush over the chipped away bark. On the trunk of the tree, he has carved "C+G tu es les étoiles de ma lune." He had been taking French for the last three years, but I'd chosen Spanish and had no idea what this said.

"What does it mean?" I ask, my fingers still caressing each of the indentations he had made. Must have taken him a while.

He brushes the back of his index finger along my jawline to my chin. "It says 'the stars to my moon,'" he whispers, although I'm the only person close enough to hear.

My face hurts from the smile he has given me. "I love you, too."

A tear rolls down my cheek and I wonder if that tree —inside the confines of our high school—still displays our initials. Or if the bark has grown and covered it over the years. The younger, lovestruck part of me wants to visit the tree again. The tree where it all began. Our tree.

Luna curls up beside me, purring with vigor as I stroke her soft fur. And after a few minutes pass, I drift off to a deep sleep where I dream about trees and love and the starry skies above.

TODAY IS the fourth day of the shoot and I am nervous as to how it will go.

Last night was one of the best times I have had in a while. We didn't do anything extravagant—a nice dinner, an ice cream cone, and a walk on the beach. Breezy conversation and a comfort that only comes with familiarity. It was better than any other night I have shared with a woman. And there is only one reason.

Cora.

Being near her again is like learning how to breathe for the first time in years. Sure, breathing happened while we were apart, but it was merely to exist until I found my way back to her. And it feels as if I have finally rediscovered her. I only hope she has managed to do the same.

During today's shoot, we are supposed to be strolling through parts of downtown Dunedin. Me in some hoity-toity outfit while Cora walks five to ten paces behind me, snapping photos of me "looking casual" on the street. Looking casual in my world translates into walking along the sidewalk and turning to look at something with your profile or whole face toward the camera. But don't look at the camera. Because looking at the camera is not natural, or so they say. Whatever.

It's all ridiculous if you ask me. But that's what the companies and consumers love. At least for this particular brand. The shoots for romance novels and risqué, they want your hungry eyes straight on. They want the consumer to feel as if you're reaching out and luring them in.

So, after my morning walk on the beach and a shower, I dress in a linen short-sleeve, white button-up, a pair of khaki cargo shorts with more pockets than I'd ever fill and a pair of boat-style shoes. And don't forget the chunky watch and dark-tint sunglasses. Each shoot's ensemble hangs in plastic wardrobe bags in my closet, labeled, courtesy of my wonderful agent.

The only part of this whole ensemble I would use again is probably the sunglasses. They mask the sun better than any pair I have owned in recent years. Lucky for me, I get to keep everything from the shoot.

Alyson and I meet in the lobby and walk to her rental

car, sliding in and driving off the beach. The shoot doesn't start for a little more than an hour, so we agreed to grab breakfast nearby.

Once we are seated and place our breakfast orders, Alyson chimes in and starts asking about last night. I expect nothing less from her.

"So, how was dinner? Anything I need to be concerned over?" A look of genuine worry pinches her brow line.

"Dinner was good. She was worried at first, because she didn't see you. But after we talked for a few, everything went well."

"And I'll ask again. Anything I need to be concerned over?" Alyson persists.

"Nope. Just two old friends, eating together and sharing good conversation." Maybe if I say it enough times, I will start believing it myself. Because Cora and I will always be more than "old friends."

"And there were no flashes going off anywhere? From your phone or anyone else's?"

"I didn't catch any. No one around here knows me as a model. The only people who know me are the few friends I have still living here." If anyone recognizes me as a model while I'm here, shocked wouldn't begin to cover it. Yes, celebrities live in the area. But this isn't Los Angeles, and people aren't stalking celebrities. Not that I consider myself one. For the most part, when people spot celebrities here, they just whisper and go on with life.

She spins her fork in a circle on her napkin. "I hope you're right."

We finish breakfast in silence, and I take the time to do a self-evaluation of how I feel.

Being around Cora stirs up loads of memories and emotions I suppressed for years. But I can't ignore how I feel when near her. The way my heart rattles my ribcage. Or how my stomach quivers with excitement. Of course, I plan to follow etiquette and maintain a professional appearance while working, but once "off the clock" I cannot speak for my actions. I also won't resist what is right in front of me.

Because each moment I have with Cora, I intend to take full advantage. This shoot could be complete happenstance. Or maybe it is kismet. Personally, I believe in the latter.

After Alyson and I leave the restaurant, we stop at the juice place up the street. Cora had one of their juices the other day, so I Googled the business. Once I buy something for each of us, even grabbing a duplicate of Cora's drink for Erin, we jump back in the car and drive up the street to the main hub of downtown.

It is eight-thirty in the morning on a Thursday, and the streets already have people walking and bicycling everywhere. Downtown Dunedin is a quaint place. I hadn't come here much when I lived in the area, but I can see I missed out.

Restaurants and boutiques and eclectic shops line the

streets. People bustle along the sidewalk, going from one shop to the next. Some people just sit on benches under trees and chat about what a nice day it is outside. And as busy as it is, it's not busy at the same time. Everyone is friendly as smiles are shared amongst complete strangers.

It's pieces of home like this that make me want to return.

Don't get me wrong. There are many stretches of California I love. Forests and mountains and waterfalls. Many I would love to show to Cora, knowing her love for the wilderness. But I haven't been anywhere resembling this. The happy town with ever happier residents. Everyone shares warm greetings and pleasant words and exchanges hugs. It makes me homesick for a place I haven't called home in a long time.

Alyson parks the car in a small lot near the epicenter of downtown and we walk over to the outdoor trail, standing in the shade. Cyclists whip past us, waving and smiling. Dogs sniff the grass as they walk alongside their owner. People window shop the storefronts nearby.

"She emailed me early this morning and said for us to meet her here," Alyson tells me.

A moment later, Cora and Erin pull into the parking lot at the same time and park beside Alyson's rental car. My eyes remain fixed on Cora behind my sunglasses as she gets out of the car and strolls to the back hatch, opening it and taking out her camera bag.

"Check yourself, Hunt," Alyson chirps behind me.

"Did I do something, *Miss Jameson*?" I curl my lip at her. She is really starting to piss me off.

"First, remember that you hired me to do exactly what it is I am doing. Second, don't take that tone with me. You will respect me." Alyson stares at me like a mother scolding a child. In some respects, she is correct. I did hire her to keep me "in line."

But she also needs to remember her place in the grand scheme of things.

"I know what I hired you to do. And since I'm the one signing your paycheck, I suggest *you* check yourself. I'm fully aware of my boundaries. And if I want to cross them, it'll be when the shoot is done. Which, by the way, is only a few days from now." I pause and lower my voice since Cora and Erin are walking our way. "I'll be here a few days after the shoot ends, I intend on enjoying that time however I see fit."

Alyson purses her lips. "You're the boss."

Damn right I am. Best you remember.

Cora and Erin step up and I hand them the juices I bought them. "Good morning, ladies. Just something to help keep you going today."

Cora's lips curve up at the corners while Erin blushes at the gift. It's just juice, not a bundle of flowers. Maybe Erin is naturally timid and the rosiness comes easily. Or there is the possibility she knows about the "meeting" last night. Whatever, it doesn't bother me either way.

I glance down at the chunky watch on my wrist to see it is just after one when we wrap up for the day. This shoot dragged out longer due to the amount of pedestrian traffic we had to avoid for photos. It's challenging to capture someone's face, and their attire, when people walk all around you.

Erin heads to her car, and Alyson to the rental. I tug on Cora's hand and keep the two of us by the trail for a minute, giving us a fraction of privacy while we talk.

"What's up?" she asks, her tone casual and light.

"Just wanted to say thanks again. For not walking away from me last night. And for hanging out. Was nice to see you outside of all this." I wave my hand around us.

"It was nice," she says as a smile softens her features. "Do you want to go out with everyone tomorrow? We're going bowling."

"I'd love to. Who's everyone?"

"Me, Erin, Shelly, and Jonas. We can ask Micah, too. If you want."

All but one of those names is familiar. "I'll text Micah and see if he wants to go. Who's Jonas?" Because I really want to know. Jonas is not the name of any female I have ever met. Micah would have told me if Shelly has a boyfriend. And Erin seems too innocent to be dating—although, I could be way off base with her.

"Jonas is a friend. He helped me try to fix my old car years ago. It had so many problems and I was a frequent shopper at the mechanic shop he works at and we just became friends. He's a nice guy. I think you'll like him."

A furnace boils in my veins as I try tapering my emotions before I say something harsh. It is not my place to play the jealous anything. I lost that privilege years before she met this Jonas person. And I know absolutely nothing about him.

But that doesn't stop my truths from surfacing.

Am I still in love with Cora? Absolutely. There is not a day of my future I foresee not loving her.

Does that give me the right to dictate who she hangs around? Nope, not one bit. If she tells me she and this Jonas character are just friends, I believe her.

So, I suck it up like a trooper and put on the smile I have been trained to use. "If you think so, I'm sure it's true." I relax my forced expression, only because she is looking at me as if she can see right through it. "Will you give me your number?"

She shakes her head for a few beats. "Why? Don't misunderstand me," she says as she jerks her head toward Alyson. Her teeth tug on her lip as she regards

Alyson's eyes on us. But I don't give a fuck. Alyson can take her sinister stares and fly them back to California.

"So I can text you after I talk with Micah." That's a perfectly sufficient reason to need her number, seeing as she asked me to join them.

"Okay." She nods and I pull out my phone.

I open up a new text and she prattles off her cell to me. When she finishes, I type a message and send it to her. Her phone chimes in her back pocket and a smile dons my face as my heart beats a little faster.

I glance up and see Alyson drilling holes through me with her eyes. Her irritation is raking my nerves. "I should head out," I tell Cora, although it's the last thing I want to do. If anything, I would love to spend the rest of the day wandering downtown, holding her hand and chatting more.

"Me, too. I'll see you tomorrow."

"See you tomorrow." I lean into her, wrap my arms around her midsection and inhale her scent. She smells so much better than I remember. The perfect blend of frankincense and gardenia. Against every fibrous desire in my body, I release her and head to the car, giving her a small wave after I get in.

Once we are out of the lot and driving back toward the hotel, Alyson decides it is time to give me her two cents. "I get that you think you know what you're doing, but please be careful. There are only two days left for the shoot. All I'm saying is to be mindful."

I opt to not respond, and the drive back to Clearwater Beach takes twice as long. But during the entire ride, Alyson's words repeat in my head.

Be mindful.

THE FIFTH DAY of the shoot comes and goes and remains uneventful. Which boggles my mind.

The shoot was on the beachside of the hotel, this time in the water. Normally, a shoot like this would be classified as simple, easy. The model is out in the water, playing amongst the waves, posing on occasion and I snap the shot. Easy peasy lemon squeezy.

But, of course, with Gavin it is the complete opposite.

The shots weren't difficult to capture. My breath, on the other hand, seemed to get lost in the breeze. My racing heart chasing on its heels.

Sitting cross-legged on my bed, I pick up my camera and remove the SD card. After inserting it in the card reader, I plug it into my laptop and download the photos. A few minutes later, my eyes are inundated with thousands of photos of Gavin in the surf. I scroll through the tiled photos, clicking on this one and that one. Some appear the same with maybe a slight angle change with his chin or eyes. Others are noticeably different.

My finger taps the trackpad and the next photo fills the screen, corner to corner. I suck in a breath at the sight before me, my eyes glued to the screen and glazing over. I can't look away. Can't stop the category five hurricane wreaking havoc on my insides.

Today's shoot started earlier than the previous days. We needed to have Gavin in the water with no one nearby. In order to do that, he was in the water as soon as the sun started rising behind us in the east. The lighting was just enough to see him and the shorts hanging low on his hips.

The photo in front of me left me speechless.

Gavin stood in the water, the surface a few inches below the waistband of the shorts. His torso slightly twisted, palms resting on top of the water outstretched, his profile staring south into the distance. The dim morning light just enough to outline his silhouette. The length of his hair hiding parts of his profile. His contours defined with glimpses of curves and valleys and sinew, and droplets of water beaded on his skin. And the sharp edge of his stubble-covered jawline.

"Wow," I whisper-gasp to myself.

This photo… consider me stunned.

Stunned by his gorgeous features, the relaxed muscles peaking and dipping and contouring in all the right places. Breathless by his form and posture in the light. Shocked by the way my chest heats and thumps vigorously at the sight of him like this. In his element and one-hundred-percent himself.

Flashes of his love for the beach wake from my memory. Not for the fine, white sands or the warm, salty water. But for the serenity it provides him. The occasional stillness mixing with absolute chaos. How the sun dips below the horizon and lights the sky in breathtaking pinks and oranges. We watched so many sunsets together before he left. No two the same. And each time, I watched him from the corner of my eye, captivated by his tranquility.

This is him. Pure and uninhibited.

And this photo may not be what the brand is looking for, but it is something I will never let go of. A piece of him. The real him. The Gavin I fell in love with all those years ago.

My finger strokes over the photo, the outline of his triceps and forearm. I sigh and drop my hand from the screen.

I am fucking hopeless. And screwed.

I save the photos to my external drive and shut down the computer. My head still in the clouds as I dream of Gavin in my life in ways he never has been. Jumping up from the bed, I startle Luna in the process.

"Sorry, Luna. Momma's head is somewhere in la-la-land right now."

I head for the bathroom and crank the hot water in the shower, praying the spray will snap me out of my thoughts. Thoughts which will more than likely lead down a fresh path of sadness and heartache. I should be trying to erase the daydreams running circles in my head, right? Erase them and replace them with Gavin's inevitable departure. The more days that pass, the closer it gets to the end of the shoot. And the sooner this dream will fade away. Because that is all this is. A dream.

The parking lot of the bowling alley is packed. I wind up and down the rows in search of a vacant space, finally parking after I hit the fourth row. Jogging up to the entrance, I spot Shelly and Micah and slow when I notice they are in a heated conversation.

As I approach, Micah notices me and stops speaking, an artificial smile marking his face.

Great. I must have been the topic they were arguing politely about.

"Hey, Micah," I say, laying the sweetness on a little thick. "Long time no see."

Shelly bounds over to me and squeezes me as if I'm her lifeblood. Micah watches us, a smirk pulling at the corner of his mouth as he mumbles something unintelligible.

What the hell is his problem?

"Just ignore him. He's pissed because he thinks you and Gavin will ruin his night of fun," Shelly tells me before sticking her tongue out at her brother.

Not quite sure how he thinks us bowling together is going to disrupt his good time. And if I'm honest, I don't really care about his feelings. I have seen Micah a couple times over the last year. About the same number of times I see him every year. And usually that is because I attend gatherings with Shelly where he happens to be also.

Whatever. He can suck it up like the thirty-one-year-old big boy he is.

"Micah," I say, snagging his attention from the parking lot. "The only person that can ruin your night is you. So…"

In all his my-best-friends-big-brother glory, he salutes me with his middle finger. Asshole. And so immature. An outsider would peg him as the youngest out of all of us.

I loop my arm in Shelly's and we skip into the bowling alley, ignoring the dipshit standing outside. We head over to the check-in counter, pay for shoes and receive our lane number. I shoot a text to Erin and Jonas, letting them know Shelly and I are inside and which lane number we are at.

Shoes laced up, Shelly and I go in search of the perfect bowling ball. When we return to the lane, Jonas is there and swapping his steel-toe boots for the snappy red and blue bowling shoes. He notices us step into the bowling circle and lifts his head up, a megawatt smile spreading his lips. I have missed his face this week.

"Hey, ladies. What time does galactic bowling begin?"

I wrap my arms around him, hugging him as hard as I normally do. "In about fifteen minutes."

Just as I release him of the hug, I hear footsteps thunder behind me. I turn to see Micah and Gavin, and before I can greet Gavin, I stop myself. The relaxed and soothing demeanor Gavin has displayed toward me all week is nowhere to be seen. Instead, it has been replaced with ego and rage and maybe a hint of jealousy.

He needs to chill the fuck out.

"Gavin," I sing, "this is Jonas. Jonas, this is Gavin."

I wait for one of them to be the bigger man and offer their hand to shake. An eternity passes before Jonas rises from the plastic bucket-style seat and offers his hand. How did I know he would be the one to extend the olive branch? Maybe because he and I don't share the same sort of history Gavin and I do.

"Hey, man. Nice to meet you. Cora's told me a little about you."

Gavin shakes his hand, his eyes sizing up Jonas in the process. "Has she now? And what, pray tell, has she told you about me?" His voice laden with sarcasm and authority and ownership.

For fuck's sake. Put your dick away, Gavin. This is not the time or place.

"Just that you guys dated in high school and she hasn't seen you in years. Until this week, of course. She said the shoot has been great, though." Jonas's tone is calm and collected. But his choice of words is meant to inflict guilt and envy.

Seriously? I do not want to be the center of some stupid pissing match. Why is it so difficult to be friends with men?

Gavin's eyes narrow and I almost see the witty comeback he works hard to deliver. Everything inside me just wants this to stop, so we can have a few drinks, eat some greasy pizza, and play hours of black light bowling.

And just when I think Gavin might keep his mouth shut, he proves me wrong.

"It has been great. Nothing like spending several hours of the day with a beautiful woman. And an evening too."

That's it. I have had it. I shove against Gavin's chest. Hard. "Okay, okay. We all get it. You both have dicks. Could you stop being one so we can have a good time? I don't plan to spend my evening defending myself against testosterone."

I watch as he stares at Jonas, jaw clenched, before he

softens his features and shifts to look at me. "Sure thing. Let's have some fun."

And before I realize what is happening, he bends down and kisses the corner of my mouth. I don't respond. No flinch. No kiss in return. Nothing.

Instead, fire ignites in my chest and radiates through every molecule in my body. Fire from feeling his lips on me again. But also because he did it to use me as a pawn. And I am no one's pawn. How can desire and anger be so in unison? I don't have the answer, but they both flood my veins like the Nile. Fuel my indignation. And slowly steal every bit of happiness I had about having a night out with friends.

I stare up into his eyes, his face a look of victory. But I am ready to slap it right off his pretty little lips.

Pressing up on my toes and leaning toward his ear, I whisper-hiss, "If you ever try to use me like I'm some sort of prize again, you'll wish you'd never returned here."

I step back and set my expression to a level so frigid he shivers. We stare at each other a minute. His eyes never leave mine. They ask me a million questions regarding me and Jonas and him. But I hold my ground. Jonas is my friend and I made that abundantly clear to him when I invited him. If he can't handle me having other men in my life, then this second chance at whatever will end faster than it began.

He nods and his lips move without sound, *I'm sorry.*

I give him a tight smile and return to my friends. Erin joined us sometime during that whole showdown. Sitting between Jonas and Erin, I watch as Shelly types names on the screen—giving each of us an alternate identity.

I have been dubbed "The Raven." Shelly "The Queen." Jonas landed "The Machine." Erin bows at "The Peacekeeper." Micah gets "The Asshole." Because that is what happens when your sister picks your name. And Gavin receives "The Dreamer."

Everyone except me questions their names and tells her to change them. The raven suits me on many levels, and the temporary nickname perks my lips. First and foremost, black is life. Second, intelligence. No doubt there are plenty more sufficient reasons, but I will just stick with those two.

Once everyone stops antagonizing Shelly about name changes, bowling balls are chosen and the game begins. Five minutes into the first game, the bright fluorescent bulbs go out and are replaced with black lights and flashing party lights. A DJ belts out of the speakers and prattles on about people coming to the booth for music requests.

The first of many remixed or electronic songs comes on and I start bopping in my seat. Erin currently rolls her ball down the lane, a sad puppy expression on her face when she turns after only knocking one pin down. My hand comes up in a *rock on* gesture and I smile at her in encouragement. Her next ball yields seven more pins and she walks away with a smile.

"That's my girl," I holler. Her beaming smile is the best response and I put my hand up for a high five.

Frames are played and pitchers of beer and greasy pizza get ordered as laughter and goofiness ensue. For the next two hours, everything goes well. No testosterone battles. No bitching. It almost feels like old times.

Until one minor touch.

I grab my ball from the return, shift into the approach area and line my feet where I typically set them. Lifting the ball, I hold it steady and study the pins in front of me. When ready, I take a left-right-left, followed by a swing back and release as I swing forward. Normally, the ball would glide off my fingers and spin down the lane, the marble pattern hypnotizing on its path to the pins.

But that is not what happens.

What actually occurs is left-right-left, swing back, a smack to the leg and a twist of the ankle as the ball flies backward. It hurts like a son of a bitch and I cry out as I crumple to the floor.

Within seconds, Jonas is at my side, asking if I am okay. When I let him know I will be fine and I just need to sit a minute, he offers to help me up. Up to this point, everything is okay and I realize this because Gavin and Micah had walked off to get more beer.

The moment I stand upright, Jonas steadies me with

both his hands resting on my shoulders, his eyes scrutinizing my face. "You sure you're good?"

"Yeah. Thanks for helping me up."

And that is when it happens. When the shit hits the fan.

Jonas brings his hand to my cheek, brushing his thumb along my cheekbone and down to my jaw. He tugs lightly on strands of my hair before swiping them behind my ear. The gesture is tender and sweet and is taken away the second Gavin is within eyeshot.

"What the fuck do you think you're doing?" Gavin rages, his hands balled into fists at his sides.

"What's your deal, man? She just hurt herself and I was helping," Jonas charges back.

Gavin takes two steps closer. "I can see you helping. Keep your fucking hands to yourself, asshole."

What the actual fuck?

"Gavin," I soothe. "Jonas was helping me. I hit my leg with the ball and fell. He was making sure I was okay and helped me stand back up. You'd know that if you were here." My voice transitions from soothing to bold to anger in a flash.

Who does he think he is? He has no hold over me. He has no right to step in and assume the role he is taking right now. That role was extinguished when he stopped calling and writing. That role was extinguished the day he abandoned me.

He steps up to me, looks me square in the eyes,

ignoring the fact that Jonas is less than two feet away. His eyes bounce back and forth between mine as he searches my face for answers. Answers to questions he has been dying to ask me, but is scared to know the truth. If he wants the truth, he will need to man up and ask what he is so desperate to know.

"Please," I beg then close my eyes. As much as I would like to continue staring into his mesmerizing eyes, I can't focus when I do. I continue speaking with my vision shielded. My voice just above a whisper. "Please stop doing this. You can't do this. You can't come back after thirteen years and act as if nothing has changed. *Everything has changed.*"

"Look at me," he whispers.

I pinch my eyes tighter a moment before opening them and refocusing on his face. His face is inches from mine, and it is both exhilarating and unnerving. In my periphery, I notice everyone has moved away from us. Even Jonas.

The music morphs to one song then another, and we stand in silence. His eyes hypnotize me more with each passing beat and I swear he is figuring out a way to imprint his soul onto mine. Little does he know, he already has.

And when his finger traces the line of my jaw, I stop breathing. My eyes close and I wish on every star I have ever seen in the night sky that he will kiss me. But he doesn't.

He leans forward, his stubbled cheek lightly scrapes against mine, and whispers in my ear. "Not everything has changed. At least not for me."

He doesn't pull away from me. His warm, cotton-covered chest presses against mine and I feel the acceleration of his breathing—on my chest and at my ear. Calloused fingers traipse, with the slightest pressure, from my upper bicep down to my elbow and follow the lines of my forearm until he reaches the tips of my fingers. His fingers leave a trail of sparks everywhere he touches me and I can't ignore the swirl of energy erupting in my body.

"Gavin…" *Fuck,* I can't breathe. Can't think.

His breath is hot on my ear. "I won't come out and say it, but my feelings for you… if anything, they've only gotten stronger."

No. No, no, no, no. He can't do this. Not now. Not after all this time.

My brain jumbles into a fog of confusion. How can this be happening? It took me years to get over him. Years. To accept that he was never coming back. To accept I would never have the same connection with another person like I did him. Accept that I would exist among my friends and become some old cat lady.

And then he waltzes back into town—although it was his job that brought him and no other reason—and acts as if it is okay to resume his role beside me. It is *not* so simple.

It sounds strange, but I mourned his loss. Literally mourned him. Laid in my bed for weeks, aside from school, and cried until the tears would no longer fall. I lost sleep over him, far too many hours to track. This went on for months. So many months it was almost a year before I stopped crying for him. But the crying wasn't the end of it. It got replaced with well-disguised depression. Depression that still lingers to this day.

I won't let myself be that girl again. He can't do this. Make me fall in love with him again and then hop on a plane and fly back to the other coast. I won't survive. Not again.

Coolness replaces the heat of his breath at my ear, but I know he hasn't shifted far because his chest still rises and falls against mine. Not knowing what I will see, I take a chance and open my eyes and am met with the softest gaze. His grays spill into me. Plead with me. Implore me. Their silky silence calls to my heart and begs me to be something more. Begs me to be vulnerable for him again. And it hurts that I want to. So much.

"You can't say that. Not to me." The harsh scrape of my own words is an unfamiliar sound to my ears.

His eyes hold mine as he weaves his fingers between my own. "Why?"

"Because you can't say things like that and then leave me," I blurt, my body trembling. "The last time you left." My voice breaks. "It took me a really long time to find myself again. And even after I did, there were still days I lapsed. If it happens again…"

His eyes darken as he studies me. If he moves two inches closer, his lips will be on mine. And as much as I long to know how it would feel again, I fear the consequences my heart will endure.

"I'm sorry how things happened last time. You *know* I had no control in that scenario. But now…" He takes my chin between his thumb and first finger. "You and I have all the control."

"Do we?" I counter. "We live almost three thousand miles apart. How do we have control?"

The pad of his thumb brushes over my lower lip, causing me to close my eyes and suck in a breath. Blood whooshes loudly in my ear. My fingers tighten around his. Adrenaline parades throughout my body as flutters swarm beneath my sternum.

"What if we didn't live so far apart?"

Red and yellow lights spin circles around us when my eyes bolt open. Hundreds of people hurl globes of plastic-resin along oil-slicked hardwood in the hopes of knocking over wooden pins. Music wails from speakers and I have zero clue as to what is playing. Our friends resumed bowling without us, presumably playing our turns when they came around.

"What?" I stumble. The question is twofold. One— did I hear him correctly? Two—is he suggesting what I think he is suggesting? That one of us moves?

"It's something I've thought about for a while now. The only reason I moved away was because I *had* to. That's not a sufficient enough reason for me to be there anymore."

My mind dizzies with his confession. Part of me is ecstatic at the possibility of him moving back to Florida. Another part of me is wary. Wary things can never go back to how they were, regardless of how either of us feels.

"But how? Your job. Friends. Life," I ramble.

His thumb strokes my lip again and he moves a breath closer. "I can do my job from anywhere. As it is, I'm almost never home. I fly somewhere new every week or two. But I've stockpiled and I can lessen how much I work. As well as be pickier about the shoots I do. The few friends I have there will understand. Believe me. And my life? It has never been in Cali. I may live there, but my life is here. Always has been."

This is too much information all at once. My free hand comes up to his bicep and I brace myself against his weight. *I can't get my hopes up. Not again. Not after last time.*

"I need to sit down," I tell him.

He helps me to a seat and squats down in front of me. The look in his eyes says three words I haven't said to another soul since he left. And right now, it is way too much.

"Tell me what you're thinking," he stammers.

I memorize his expression and then drop my head in my hands. "I'm thinking this is going to slay me in the end. That I'll wither and crumble."

His fingers play with the strands of my hair that cover my hands. It is a balm to the conflicting emotions that spiral around my heart. And I temporarily relish in the feel of such an intimate gesture.

"I won't let that happen," he promises.

My head jerks up. "How can you be certain? How can you make such a colossal vow?"

His eyes lock on mine, assurance backing his words. "Because it's the only thing I've wanted since I was forced to leave you. Cora…" he says as he strokes a hand down the side of my face. "You are everything to me. You are the reason I breathe."

I drop my head back into my hands, hiding my face from the world and convincing myself not to cry. After a few minutes, I inhale deeply and force myself upright. When I check the time, I realize an hour has passed and guilt washes over me at how I have abandoned my friends.

"We need to continue this conversation, but not now. Right now, I need to drink more and throw a ten-pound ball. I need to hang out with my friends. Okay?"

He nods and stands up in front of me. "Okay," he whispers as he kisses the top of my head.

We turn back to the group and talk with everyone. The night has morphed into an awkward ball of tension.

No one is sure how they should act or what to say. But I do my best to ignore the weirdness and continue bowling and drinking.

But when the night ends, everyone is quick to leave. Too quick. And, unfortunate for me, I am too inebriated to drive and Gavin is the only person standing beside me.

Fuck. My. Life.

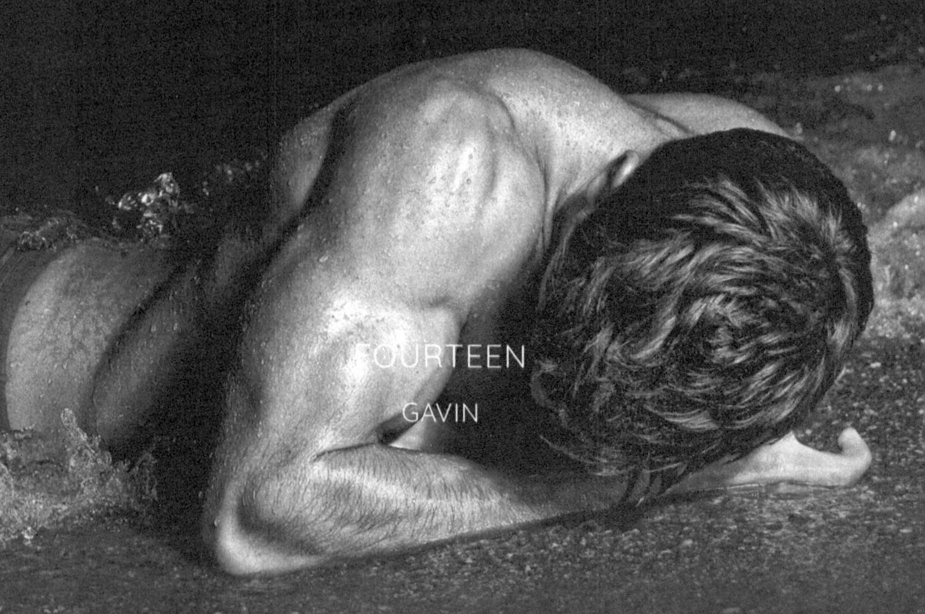

SINCE I TOOK an Uber to the bowling alley, I assumed I would leave with Micah. Assumed he and I would hang after. But that is not how things happened. Instead, Micah changed his shoes and headed out without a word. When I shot him a text to check on him, his response was lackluster.

Micah: We'll catch up another time bro.

Lame. But after the whole debacle in the bowling alley, I don't blame him. And I am a shitty friend for ignoring him most of the night. Something I need to correct. But not now.

Because now I am driving Cora's car and following her slurred directions. Toward her house. Just me and her. Alone. And my nerves zap like live wires.

Not so sure this is the best idea. But there was no way in hell I would let her get behind the wheel when she consumed close to a pitcher of beer after our talk. Erin or Shelly could have driven her home, but then she would have had to worry about her car tomorrow.

It is easier for me to drop her home and catch an Uber back to the hotel. To make sure she gets home safely. To make sure she gets inside and locks the door. At least that is what I keep telling myself.

She slurs from the passenger seat as she points like a madwoman at the exit sign. "Take exit Drew. Snot so much traffic," she snorts. "I said snot."

I shake my head and laugh at her. The last time I saw her, we were too young to drink. Not that age stops people from drinking alcohol, but we didn't back then. Seeing her like this, I'm not quite sure how I feel about it.

Is this a normal thing for her? Going out with her friends and getting hammered. Does she drink heavily and drive after? Does she get wasted with that Jonas prick around? My blood boils at the idea. Has he tried to make a move on her while she was tipsy or drunk?

Fuck.

Just the thought of her with another guy pisses me off. Not like I expected her to not move on or see other people after everything. Hell, I did my best to soothe my crippled heart. Had meaningless sex with countless women. Tried to date. None of it stuck, though.

But seeing another man near Cora—his interest in her

far beyond friendship—was a smack in the face. My blood turned molten and I was pumped and ready to kick his ass. If she hadn't been there to stop me, I probably would have and regretted it later.

What intrigues me most is how Cora thinks this Jonas prick only wants to be friends with her. Is she blind to the way he looks at her? Or how eager he is to touch her? Their hug earlier… the way he stroked her cheek and hair after she fell… *Fuck.* Either she is oblivious or doesn't want to believe.

I can't let these thoughts fester inside me. I need to know what sort of relationship exists between Cora and this Jonas guy. She doesn't owe me anything, and I would be shocked if she answers me, but I have to ask.

"Hey," I start, and she looks over at me. "What's up with you and this Jonas guy?"

She tilts her head to the side and remains silent in the passenger seat. After a minute, she starts laughing. At first, it is her typical laugh, but then it morphs into hysterics and snort-laughing. And then she laughs at her own snort-laughing. It's kind of cute.

This goes on for another minute until she tells me to turn left at the next light. We take a left and another left a couple blocks later. Less than a quarter mile later and we are parked in her driveway.

She still hasn't answered my question and I wonder if she even remembers I asked it. We sit in silence after I cut the engine and neither of us moves to get out.

"He's just a friend," she whispers into the quiet, her voice somber. "I know he wants to be more than friends, and it's crossed my mind on occasion, but we've been friends too long to ruin it. At least that's my opinion."

She sounds more sober than she did fifteen minutes ago and I wonder if it is the topic at hand or if she wasn't that drunk to begin with. I don't plan on asking her. But if she will keep talking, I will probe for more.

"If he asked you," I hesitate, unsure if I want to know her truth. I search her eyes, wondering if she can read me in the darkness of the car. Her eyes used to read me like a book. She knew all my answers before I did. Knew all my tells. "If he asked you, would you guys be together?"

Her silhouette is all I see in the car as a light on the back of her house casts an aura around her. I am unable to see what she thinks, but I *feel* her eyes scan over every part of my face. Look into the windows of my soul. Wonder what would provoke me to ask her. Memorize the curves along my cheekbones in search for a twitch or indication of doubt. She studies the line of my jaw and waits for me to speak more. I may not be able to see her face, but with the angle of the light I know she sees mine.

She reaches toward me, finds my hand in the dark and wraps it in hers. "I... I don't think so," she whispers, her words clear. "He's a great guy and has been a good friend. It's just..." She shakes her head. "Relationships and me haven't had the best of luck in my adult life. So, I just do the friend thing with sporadic dating. But never the same guy for more than one date."

Shit. Did I do this to her? Did I ruin love for her? God, I hope she is not like this because of me. The selfish part of me jumps up and down in victory. But the selfless part of me, he stands in the corner with a baseball bat, beating the shit out of himself.

"I'm sorry," I say the words before I stop myself.

"For what? Ruining me for every other man in the world. Don't be sorry. I don't want or need your pity. If I wanted to, I could have dated more and been in a solid relationship. But I get to decide. Is it such a bad thing to be picky? Especially after your soul has been crushed by the one person who was supposed to protect it."

Slap. Fuck, that stings. But I sure as shit deserve it.

"Can I walk you in?" I ask, wanting to steer us away from talking about this now. Not when I know she's not sober. Not when we can't discuss what happened rationally.

"What? That's it? You're done talking about it, so conversation over?"

She shoves her door open and gets out, slamming the door behind her. I rush to get out, to catch up to her before she gets inside. Halfway to her back door, I catch her wrist in my grip.

"No. That's not it at all. I just don't think we should be having this discussion when you're not one-hundred-percent coherent."

She huffs, trying to yank her arm from my hand. "You're ridiculous. You bring up the topic of discussion, but when it gets too thick… conversation done. It makes me dizzy."

She sways and I want to tell her it's not the conversation making her dizzy. But I don't because she is already pissed at me. Yanking her arm, I release her wrist and she wobbles to the door, me on her heels.

I hand her the key ring with three keys and she unlocks the door. As she steps through the door, I go to follow her and she stops.

"What are you doing?"

"It's late. Can I sleep on your couch? I won't bother you and I'll leave in the morning. If not, I'll find a ride."

Her eyes wobble a little as she studies my face. After a few breaths, she nods. "Couch." It's all she says as she walks toward a door I can only assume is her bedroom.

"Thanks," I whisper into the darkness.

Walking slowly through her quaint house, I locate the couch and kick off my shoes. I check my watch and realize it is really fucking late. Or is it really fucking early at this point? Whatever. Thank God tomorrow is an off day for the shoot. Because both of us would be fucked if it wasn't.

I stretch out on the couch, situating pillows and a blanket around me. Shifting my hips and my neck until I get comfortable. Am I really in her house? Or is this all just some bizarre dream? It all seems so surreal. Seeing her again. Touching her again. Smelling her again. Fuck, how I have missed everything about her. Even the way she says my name.

Her adorable smile. The subtle fragrance she wears. How she peers up at me. The way her body reacts to mine. As if no time has passed.

But it has. And I fucked up. Big time.

Staring up at the ceiling, my eyes lose focus as the moonlight casts shadows from the tree outside the window. Shadows of limbs and leaves dance and entertain me. Tonight, so many things have happened and changed. It's overwhelming to think of how life and our relationship could possibly shift in the future. Shift in a positive way.

The future… something I always dreamed I would have with Cora, but wasn't sure would happen. I wasn't sure I would ever see her again, but wished for it often. Wished on every star in the night sky. Wished with every penny I threw in a fountain. And wished every time I blew out a birthday candle.

When I boarded the plane in Los Angeles, the possibility of seeing her seemed minuscule. So outlandish. So impossible.

But fate intervened. Slapping us together and giving us the opportunity to discover each other again. To learn about all the years we missed out on. Learn how much we have changed yet remained the same. And now that things are lining up for both of us in our respective careers, the possibility of a future with her has greater potential. If a future with me is what she wants.

Please let it be what she wants.

If she would be willing to try with me again—if she gave me a chance to explain—I would move my life back here again. Back home. To her. For her. In a heartbeat. Regardless of my life and family and friends back in California, I would leave it all behind if I knew we stood a chance.

The day I was forced to tell her my mom received a promotion and we were moving out of state was the day my life started falling apart. One speck at a time. When my mom told me the news, I hesitated to tell Cora. Not because I didn't want to, but because when I did tell her, reality would hit hard. And when I shared the news with her, expressing the pain and anguish I felt at leaving, she held me and soothed me. She was the strong one, telling me we would be apart for less than two years. That we would see each other during breaks and summer. Less than two years and we could be by each other's side again.

We had it all mapped out.

Unfortunately for us, it didn't work that way. Within ten days of being in California, my life was utter chaos. Upset and angry, I lashed out. Got in fights and provoked anyone near me. I think a part of me thought if I acted out, I would be able to return to where I wanted to be most. Where I belonged. With Cora.

But it didn't work that way and I shut down. To my family and Cora. I allowed my anger and frustration and sadness to consume me until numbness took over. A numbness that pushed me forward, but I lost every real part of who I had been. Including Cora.

It may have taken thirteen years for me to return—by complete accident—but I am here. And I plan to do whatever it takes to regain all I have lost. I will make up for every tear she cried. Every sadness she suffered. I will make up for every pain and absence of love she has endured since I left. She deserves nothing less from me.

I surveil the shadows as they continue to sway and, within minutes, I drift off and hope I dream about the most incredible woman I have ever loved. The woman who sleeps less than twenty feet from me. The woman I hope will forgive me in the end. And somehow, love me again.

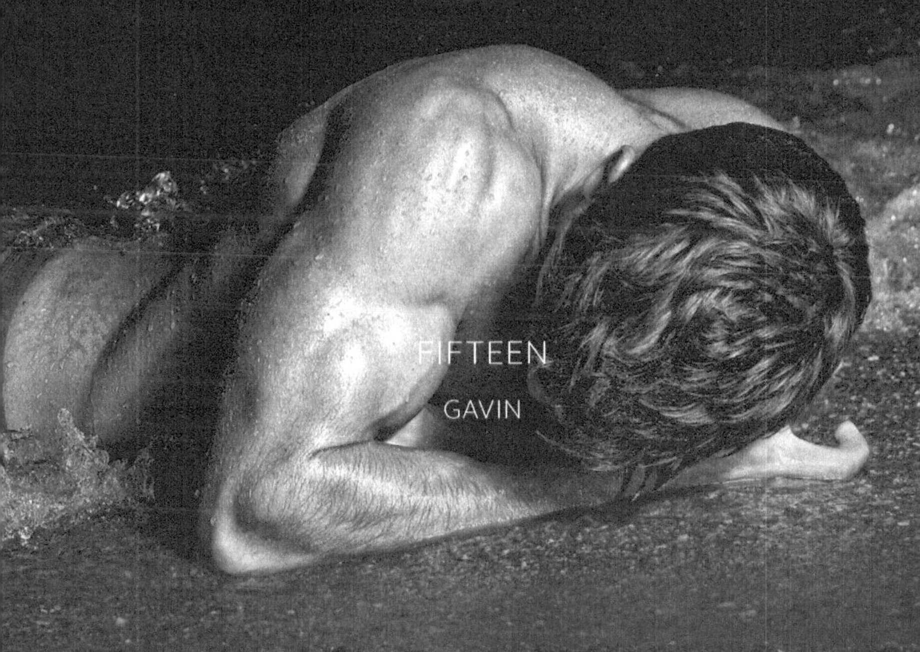

FIFTEEN

GAVIN

Fifteen years ago

I JUMP out of the bus and land on the concrete sidewalk of my new school. *High school. I am in the big leagues now. No stopping me.*

Freshman year holds so much promise. Making new friends. Meeting new people. Hot new females. Life couldn't possibly get any better.

I toss my backpack over one shoulder and head for the class where my homeroom is said to be. The first day is usually full of chaos, and today is no exception. Even though it is corny as hell, I am glad my mom forced me to come to orientation so I at least got a lay of the land. The last thing I need is to look like a dope wandering the halls while staring at a map.

Navigating the hall, I locate the correct room and find

a desk in the back row. There is still another six minutes until the bell, so I pull out my notebook and begin doodling while I wait. Stomps and thuds and soft pitter-patters echo off the sterile white walls as everyone files into the room. I ignore all their steps and continue my artwork, the buzzing of the bell causing me to stop.

When I peer up at the front of the room, a raven-haired girl walks through the door, huffing and bending at the waist as she tries to catch her breath. Her skin is pale as cream, her onyx hair as bold of a contrast as her bloodred lips. She reminds me of a modern-day, punk rock version of Snow White, except with shorter hair. And I immediately like everything about her.

When her breath catches enough, she stands and wanders through the rows of desks, picking an available seat two over from me. I try not to stare at her, but can't help how she has caught my eye. Surely, she has caught the eye of many others as well. And not just because of her entrance. Everything about her is bewitching.

I avert my gaze when the teacher introduces himself and begins going over some of the basic school rules and hands out paperwork for our parents, the code of conduct, and our class schedules. Typical first day of school stuff. I scan over my class schedule, check I was assigned all the appropriate classes, and then wonder what classes the raven-haired girl has. Hopeful we will have at least one or more classes together.

The bell sounds and I sidle up beside her, trying to spark a conversation.

"Hey," I say with a wave. "I'm Gavin. Crazy morning?"

She glances over at me, confused. "Hi," she mumbles. "Cora. And yes."

Maybe she isn't a morning person? Or maybe she is not having the best morning. Whatever.

"Sorry to hear. Anything I can do to help?" Why not offer, right? No harm, no foul.

"Gavin, is it?" I nod. "Thanks, but I'm good," she says with a brush-off.

But I don't back down so easily. Something about her begs me to keep trying. "Well, let me know," I offer with a smile.

When she walks away, I check to see which class I head to first and make my way to the science wing. Honestly, who thinks it is a good idea for people to learn science this early in the morning?

Slap.

My geometry book closes too loud in the room and several sets of eyes stare at me like I am their next meal.

Sorry. Why does everyone seem so touchy today? *Just brush it off, man.* No one likes the first day of school. Actually, no one cares for school on any day. But no one needs to bite my head off.

I shoulder my backpack and head to the cafeteria. After I load up a tray of random crap food, I head out to the tables in the sun. The summer heat still blazes, but I would rather be outside than in the dank cafeteria. The cafeteria feels claustrophobic and I question the cleanliness.

When I step out and search for a good place to sit, I spot her. The raven-haired girl with bright red lips. Cora. She sits under a tree, eating a sandwich and reading a book. Before I realize what I am doing, I trudge over and stop in front of her. She ignores me for a few seconds, bookmarks her page, and finally looks up.

Shielding her eyes with her hands, she squints and tilts her head to the side. "Can I help you with something?"

"Mind if I sit with you?"

"Gavin... right?" I nod at her. "Well, Gavin, I'm kind of a loner."

It is not a denial, only a statement meant to scare me away. But it won't work on me. If anything, the attempt at a brush-off has me wanting to sit with her more. Cora... what a fascinating creature.

"We don't have to talk. I'm just here for the tree," I joke.

She shakes her head in disbelief, a subtle laugh under her breath as she gestures to the landscape beside her. "It's not my tree."

I squat down and manage to sit cross-legged without dropping anything from my tray. *Thanks to whoever is looking out for me so I don't embarrass myself in front of this girl.*

We sit in companionable silence—me munching on the cafeteria's mystery casserole and her eating a banana while reading *Wuthering Heights*. The book tattered and well-loved—cover curling and faded, multiple pages dog-eared.

Part of me wonders if she is reading the book for school or pleasure. My bet is on the latter considering the appearance of the novel. Can't say I have ever read the book. I'm sure it is good, but reading isn't much of a priority for me. Haven't heard of anything noteworthy.

After finishing the semi-decent casserole, I finish off my bottled water. Although our silence under the tree has been enjoyable, I itch to talk with this girl. Spark some form of conversation. Get to know the girl with the bright red lips. But she doesn't seem like the type of person who fills space with meaningless conversation. Part of me is intimidated by this. Another part of me enchanted. What do I say to someone like her?

So, I aim for obvious.

"Good book?" I ask, smacking myself upside the head internally.

Of course it is a good book, dumbass! Otherwise, it wouldn't look like she has read it a hundred times. Idiot.

She finishes the sentence or paragraph she is reading and faces me, a slight hint of annoyance on her face. It both frightens and intrigues me. "Yes." It is all she says before turning back to the book and ignoring me again.

Okay…

I stay under the tree with her for a few more minutes before rising to take my tray back to the cafeteria. After I dump the trash and deposit the tray in the bin, I turn to catch one more glimpse of her before heading to my next class. But the moment I look, she is no longer there. A strange sadness takes hold, but I brush it off.

"I'll try again tomorrow," I mumble to myself.

The art quad is located at the back of campus, on the farthest outskirts. As if sketching and paints and clays need their own world away from the books and projectors and regimented studies. As odd as it is to be isolated at the back of the school, I enjoy the fact I won't hear anything else on campus while in this class.

Walking into the large and open classroom, I scan all the various projects the teacher has kept throughout the years. Oils and watercolors, charcoals and pencil. Each unique on their own. The air rich with canvas and pencil shavings and earth. As my eyes follow around the room, they stop when they spot a head of black-as-night hair.

Cora sits at one of a dozen long, rectangular tables. Her head down as her fingers draw vigorously on a sketch pad. Almost like the artist version of a mad scientist. No one sits beside her, so I gather myself and head for the table. Of all the classes I could share with her, art feels beyond perfect. A way to express yourself without speaking.

When I sit down beside her, my wooden stool squeaking against the linoleum floor, she doesn't move. Doesn't lift her head or greet me. She is so focused on what is in front of her, it's as if the rest of the world isn't really here. And a part of me kind of digs her level of concentration.

Seconds pass and her head remains down, hovering six inches above the table. I peer around her hunched body and sneak a peek at what she sketches, my eyes widening and breath falling short as I see it come to life.

The trunk of a tree. Shade and foliage hovering above. A raven-haired girl, her face hidden by an open book. And a boy. Taller than her, lean in stature. He watches her from the corner of his eye, a timid smile on his face.

It's her. *And me.*

A strange contentment washes over me. Although the image is nowhere near done—no shading or fine lines and details—the outlines are all in black and white. She abandoned the tree early to come draw the two of us beneath it. My stomach is sort of queasy, and I don't think it is from the mystery casserole.

How has she put this on paper so quickly?

And it occurs to me. Maybe she had previously drawn herself alone under a tree. She did say she was a loner. Five minutes was definitely not enough time to have this much detail on paper. Not even by the best.

The bell rings and I inspect another twenty bodies in the room, all seated at the other tables. Footsteps tick on the tile and the teacher walks to the front of the room. But I don't look at the five foot, four inch red-haired woman at the head of the room introducing herself as the art teacher.

Because just as the teacher begins speaking, Cora lifts her head and realizes I'm sitting beside her. And that I have seen her drawing. Her face is stoic and as unreadable as a professional poker player.

A smile breaches my lips and I face the teacher at the head of the room. Beside me, I hear the sketchbook close and a soft sigh. A sigh I will remember for the rest of my days.

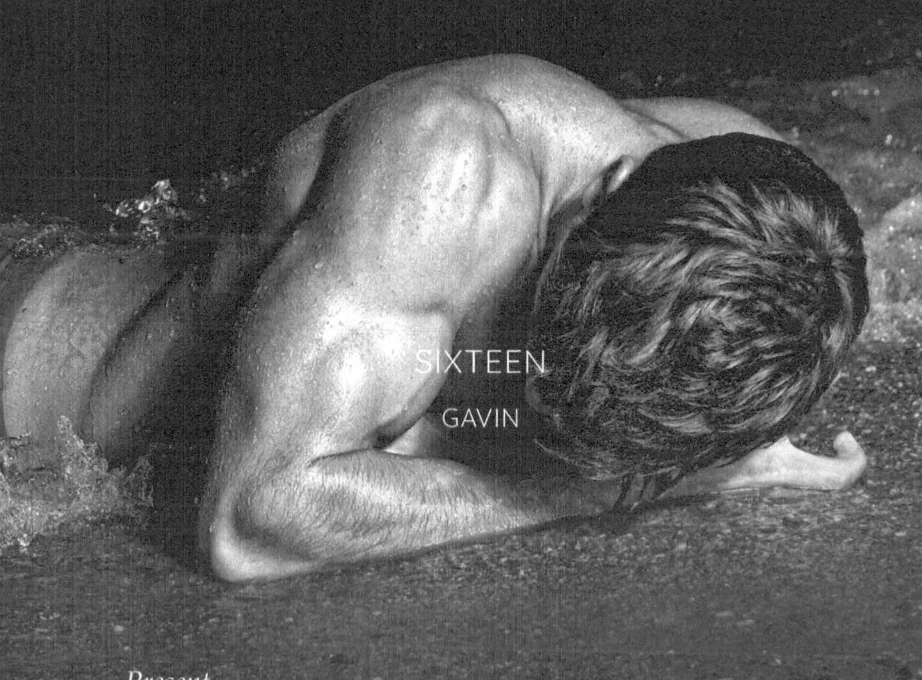

SIXTEEN

GAVIN

Present

THE SUN WAKES me up just before seven, although sections of the house remain somewhat dark. Cora still sleeps and the house is quiet. Too quiet. As if no noise exists here. Seems odd to have no noise. No cars driving by. No people talking outside. Not even the chirp of birds in the early morning light.

I should leave. The last thing I need is for Cora to wake up, find me in her house and not remember why I am here in the first place. All it would do is freak her out and set us back. When it comes to Cora, I need all the forward momentum possible.

Rising from the couch, I stretch out my limbs then fold the blanket and drape it over the couch. I tiptoe through the house in search of the bathroom. After I relieve myself, I wash up and tiptoe back out.

Finding a piece of paper and pen on the desk nestled between the living and dining area, I write a quick note. As I set the pen back in its place, I bump the corner of her open laptop and the screen lights up.

Shit.

Snagging the note, I go to close the lid of the laptop and hide its bright light. But just as I begin to push the top down, I see a photo from one of our shoots this week. A photo she left open. A photo of me.

Confusion flickers in my veins. Rapid-fire questions pop up left and right. Was the photo left open because of work and editing? Or was it left open for other reasons?

A strange, woozy sensation floats in my chest at the possibility of her ogling a photo of me. Of her sitting in this very spot and gawking at my images. But I shut down the idea, not wanting my hopes to get the best of me.

I ignore the laptop and leave it open since it will return to sleep mode within minutes.

Walking over to her bedroom door, I stand in front of it and close my eyes. Do I go in and leave the note where I know she will find it? Or should I slip it under the door? This isn't my house. And technically, Cora isn't my girl.

My internal battle continues a minute before I choose the obvious path.

I slowly twist the knob and am thankful the door stays silent as it opens. Padding through the room darkened by black-out curtains, I walk toward her bed and set the note on top of her phone. A place I know she will find it.

Before turning to leave, I stare down at her a moment. Although I should leave now, the selfish part of me stays to observe Cora without distraction. To take in the woman who has held my heart captive most of my life.

And for a moment, I study the lines of her face as she sleeps. How her brows arch up, not in the middle but closer to a lateral point. The way her long lashes fan across the purple half-moons beneath her eyes. How her black strands splay across the dark gray cotton pillowcase.

A red tank covers her chest, but rises up her midriff to unintentionally display her navel. A small locket rests atop her shirt, and I remember it as the one her mom gave her. The sheet bunches near the thick band of her underwear. Her body askew on the mattress, taking up half of the queen-size space like a giant starfish.

A contented sigh leaves my lips as I pivot to leave the room. As much as I would like to stay, now is not the day. After closing the door behind me, I retrieve my phone from the living room and head for the door. I lock the handle as I step out the back. Scanning the street, I try to orient myself and figure out where I am.

Across the street from Cora's house is a large, open

park. Honestly, doesn't surprise me she purchased a home within fifty-feet of a park. I cross the street, land on a small paved path and wander through the greenery in the faint morning light.

It is peaceful here. Most of this side of the park is filled with lush oak trees and a pathway for leisurely strolls. No wonder it was so quiet in her house.

I stand near the edge of a pond in the center of the park and watch a raft of ducks as they splash and quack and say good morning to each other. Squirrels dig at the earth in search of hidden food. A gentle breeze blows off the water, cuts the morning heat and rustles the leaves. A few people pass by with dogs and wave as if I live in the neighborhood. Everything about this place is quaint and chill and absolutely perfect.

After fifteen minutes of wandering the park and collecting my thoughts, I locate a bench on the outskirts and request an Uber. I pluck a twig from the ground, twirl it between my fingers and zone out while I wait.

Thank God I have today to myself. After everything last night, I need the time. To think and map out what happens next. Because after last night, I won't deny myself or Cora. Not again.

SEVENTEEN

CORA

SOMETHING WET SCRAPES over my nose. My cheek. My eye. It stops after a minute, but starts up again. My eyebrow. The corner of my mouth. Then my ear. Argh! *What the hell is that?* I swat at the air and come in contact with a bulky body of fur.

Luna.

She paws my face, a sweet and pleading meow only inches from my ear. When I don't respond, she paws me again and meows louder. It is a scratchy-whiny meow. One that tells me it is past time to wake up. One that tells me I need to pay her attention.

Grr... I shove her to the side and scoot to sit up. Luna rubs the side of her body against my arm, doing a figure eight and coming back for more, a noticeable purr echoing in the darkness. Giving her a light pat and a few pets, I creep out from under the sheet.

"Come on pretty girl. Let's get you some breakfast." As soon as the word breakfast is said, her cries morph into a frenzy as if I never feed her. Ridiculous, but adorable.

When she hops off the bed, I reach for my phone and pick up a piece of paper resting atop it. I pinch my eyes together in the darkness and see it is a note from Gavin.

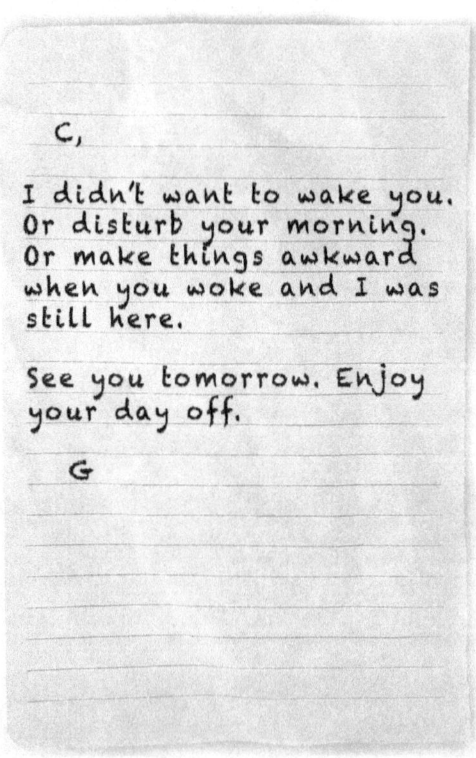

I flip the paper over as if looking for more. Or him. But find neither. No more words. No Gavin.

After drinking far too much last night, things are a bit foggy. I walk to the kitchen and pour some food into Luna's bowl before grabbing a glass of water. His note still in my hand, I walk over to the couch and plop down, a waft of his beachy pine scent hits my nose and I close my eyes as I inhale deeply.

I am so very fucked.

I reread the note a few times, trying to find some hidden meaning in his words. But nothing stands out. There is no hidden agenda. No secret meaning. It is just Gavin being Gavin.

I tip my head back and stare at the ceiling. Stare at the minor imperfections and connect them like constellations. Which makes me think of stars and night skies and sunsets. *Ugh.*

No way I can sit in this house all day. If I stare at the walls, my mind will keep venturing off into uncharted waters. Waters that always circle back to Gavin. I need to get out and do something. Anything. Maybe have a girl's day with Shelly. Watch some memorable karaoke and eat fried foods with her and Jonas. Like we always do.

Rising from the couch, I go snag my phone from the charger and shoot a text to Shelly.

Cora: Got plans today?

Not sure what her work schedule is since it fluctuates week to week, but fingers crossed we can hang today. I just need to get out of my head. And in order to do that, I need distractions and meaningless conversation.

Shelly: Off work soon. What's up?
Cora: Hang out when you're done?
Shelly: I'm down. 2:00ish good?
Cora: I'll be ready. See you soon.

Happy to have a planned distraction, I eat a yogurt with granola before heading to the shower. As I wash away everything that happened last night—professed feelings back out in the open and slapped across my friends' faces—I make a vow to myself.

I will not fall in love with Gavin Hunt. *Again.* I will not. Or at least that is what I keep telling myself.

"How's it look?" Shelly asks through the fitting room door.

I stare at myself in the wide, full-length mirror and wonder what the hell I am doing. *Being a goddamn idiot is what I'm doing.*

My fingers toy with the black lacy boy short underwear, my eyes glued to the bra—also lacy, but resembling that of a leather cage. If I really want to, I can snap a few clips and the two undergarments connect and resemble a vixen-like leotard.

"Uh… I like it. I think."

Actually, I love it. Shelly doesn't need to know that, though. But why the hell would I need to buy lingerie like this? Not as if I have someone to wear it for. And I haven't stepped foot in a club in years—the only other place I might wear something like this.

I stare at myself in the mirror as I fiddle with the lace under my fingertips.

Not as if I need clarity to strike, but let's be honest. I know why I want to buy this. Want to wear it. The exact reason. The one person who has infiltrated my thoughts since the beginning of the week is said reason. Gavin. I picked up this sexy-as-hell lingerie set because I was thinking about him when we walked past the table. Part of me snatched it because it is black and punk and risqué. Another part of me is optimistic I will have a reason to wear it.

Many women wear sexy lingerie because it provides an air of power. Even if no one else sees it, they come alive with the provocative attire on their skin.

"You think? How can you not know? Let me see," Shelly insists. And before I realize what is happening, the fitting room door opens and she steps in.

"What are you doing?" I whisper-yell.

"If you didn't want me coming in, you should've locked the door."

"Lesson learned," I mumble.

Shelly's eyes sweep over the racy ensemble before a low whistle leaves her lips.

Her scrutiny isn't uncomfortable or awkward. Neither is the fact that she stands in a five-by-five dressing room with me while I wear next to nothing and she ogles my semi-naked body. We have been friends long enough to have more of a sister bond than anything else. That is not to say we didn't share the curiosity phase in our younger years. But that was all it was for both of us, curiosity.

"He'll love it." She claps her hands together, a wicked gleam dancing on her face.

"Who?" Confusion laces my tone as I cock my head and stare at my best friend.

"Gavin," she says, looking at me as if I have two heads for questioning her comment. "He *is* the reason you're trying this on. Right? I mean, I know you're unique in many ways, but no woman tries on lingerie like this unless she has a reason."

Of course she is right, but I will not admit it. Not to her and not aloud. Geez. When did I become such a hot mess of confusion? Oh, I know. Since the moment I heard his voice drift into that banquet room. The logical side of me gets up in my face and screams. She tells me to finish this shoot and act as if he never stepped foot back in Florida.

But the rest of me… she is off traipsing along the beach, holding hands with the only person she has ever loved. The only person who stripped her bare and shattered her to pieces.

No, I refuse to be that lost, melancholy girl again. Downright refuse.

"Get out," I mutter. "I need to change."

Shelly registers the shift in my demeanor and steps out of the fitting room. When the door clicks shut, I take one last look at the siren lingerie on my body before stripping it off and tossing it to the side. After I redress, I leave the room and hand the lingerie to the attendant, thanking her.

"Not buying it?" Shelly asks, a sorrowful look aimed my way.

"No. I have no reason to."

And that sad, lonely truth hits me harder with each step as we exit the store.

EIGHTEEN

CORA

Fifteen years ago

THREE WEEKS HAVE PASSED since the first time Gavin sat next to me under the oak tree at school. Three weeks and we had become friends. Good friends. So good, we spend time together outside of school.

Gavin has even become a close runner up in the best friend department. Shelly will always take the lead. But after the first day, after he saw me adding his frame to my loner girl drawing, it had been nothing except uphill.

Besides hanging at lunch, we saw each other in art and English. Our conversations started off basic, discussing our family life and what we liked doing outside of school. Gavin seems to love art as much as I do, but swears his talents are nowhere as amazing as mine. Only time will tell that truth. We also like similar genres of movies.

By the end of the first week of school, I learned about his love for fish tacos, the beach, music, and sunsets. He told me a great day involved all four and the thought makes me smile at how easily they could be done together.

I lean against the wide trunk of the oak tree. *Our tree.* Retrieving the baby carrots and hummus from my bag, I start snacking as I flip through my book and wait for Gavin to join me. A page and a half later, he sits beside me and grumbles under his breath.

"You okay?" I ask and pause reading my book when I notice the firm pout on his face. His pouty face is kind of cute.

"Yeah. Just a little turned off by this tuna noodle casserole they're serving today. It's gnarly looking." His pouty face resumes and I bite my lip to stop myself from laughing.

"News flash, Gavin. All the cafeteria food is gnarly looking. Why do you think I bring my own food?"

He pokes his fork at the pale, goopy casserole and pushes it to all corners of the tray. As if spreading it out will magically make it more appealing.

"I might have to start waking up ten minutes earlier, so I can make something. Or..." He peeks over at me with a shit-eating grin. "You could always make lunch for both of us. I'll pay you instead of the school."

I toss a carrot at him. "I'm not your mama, boy," I tease.

He catches the carrot, sets his tray on the ground, and pops the snack in his mouth. But what I don't expect is when he starts reaching for more of my food, play fighting with me as I try to push him away. This happens for a couple minutes—him trying to steal my food, me defending my territory. We both laugh and taunt each other.

But then something shifts.

His playfulness stops when he knocks me to the ground and hovers inches above me. Carrots forgotten. Steely-gray eyes pierce mine and my breath hitches. If he lowers himself a few more inches, his lips would touch mine. And this fact heats parts of me I didn't know existed. Like I have a new organ named Gavin.

I want him to kiss me.

Only two boys have kissed me before. Greg Barton and Jeremy Ashford. Greg, two years ago. And Jeremy last school year.

Greg Barton is a year older than me and I thought kissing him would be life-altering. And it was, just not in the way I had hoped. It actually grossed me out. He had kissed me sloppily, his saliva-coated lips and tongue painting my mouth like they had no idea *where* my mouth was. I never kissed him back because the thought terrified me.

Jeremy Ashford went to middle school with me and

was the most popular boy in the school. I was so nervous just before we kissed. Probably because we were at a friend's party playing truth or dare. He was dared to kiss me. Poor guy. I still feel bad for him and the bite I'd given his tongue when he pushed it between my lips.

Needless to say, after my most recent experience, rumors spread about how I didn't know how to kiss or make out. And everyone consoled Jeremy and his marred tongue. Whatever. He was a douche. Besides, I always did better on my own. Loner girl and all.

But looking into Gavin's eyes above mine, his lips separated just enough for him to draw in breath, I know kissing him would be different. Not another awkward kiss to add to the list of strange life experiences. But maybe on another list. One where you write down all the things you never want to forget because nothing else will compare.

We may have only met three weeks ago, but Gavin is not like every other guy. And I don't know how that makes me feel.

His body presses heavier into my belly and chest, his lips a breath from mine. I close my eyes, sending a message to the gods above and thanking them for whatever is happening. My breath hitches again in anticipation and then he is gone. His weight removed from my body and the warm breeze blowing my hair in my face.

My eyes fly open and glance over to where he sits up,

a gleam of pure joy smeared across his face as he pops a carrot in his mouth.

Did he only want the stupid carrot? Or did he want to kiss me too?

Rising up from the ground, I tackle him and reach for my stolen lunch. It's not long before we share my food and his tray of scary casserole is long forgotten. We munch on veggies and hummus, and I share half of my cashew butter and banana sandwich with him. We share jokes and laugh. And I promise to make him lunch every day, as long as he foots the cost.

But when we walk away from our tree today, a new sensation flutters inside me. A new wish to be fulfilled. A desire to be kissed by the boy walking beside me.

NINETEEN

CORA

Present

"ANOTHER ROUND?" the server asks as she deposits loaded fries, onion rings, and our specified burgers on the table.

"Please," I tell her as I stuff the veggie burger between my lips.

I glance over at the stage and wish karaoke grandpa was doing his number up there. Could really use the laugh. Instead, I am forced to watch some fifty-something guy going through a midlife crisis. He practically makes out with the microphone—*I hope someone sanitizes that thing before anyone else uses it*—while he sings "Every Rose Has Its Thorns" by Poison.

...and I think his tongue just grazed the mic. Ew!

Our table is momentarily quiet as the four of us scarf

down our burgers, occasionally snatching an onion ring or fry. When I come up for air, I notice I have three sets of eyes on me. Erin, Shelly, and Jonas each drill their own hole into my skull, mining for details of why I am acting off. Their weighted stares like an unannounced party in my head. Shelly and I spent the afternoon together, so her matched stares can take a pill.

Personally, I always think I'm strange. So, I don't know what their deal is.

"I wish you would've invited me shopping earlier," Erin speaks up, bringing conversation back to the table.

"Sorry," I confess. "I didn't purposely exclude you. Just wasn't thinking straight. Guess my brain was still a little foggy from drinking too much last night." Amongst other things. But I am not announcing that to the table.

To be honest, my day out with Shelly didn't clear any of the fog either. Not like I hoped it would. Every store we passed, something caught my eye and sent my thought train Gavin's direction. It's only been a matter of days, yet he consumes every part of my day. Even now, while I sit with three of my friends and try to have a night of fun.

"It's okay. Next time," she indicates.

"Next time," I promise.

Another round of silence ensues as the woe-is-me guy leaves the karaoke stage. I cross my fingers under the table, hoping the next person is better and more upbeat. And as I watch a pair of ladies walk up to the stage, each grabbing a mic and whispering to each other before the music kicks in, I hope my prayers will be answered.

Seconds later, "Bootylicious" by Destiny's Child crackles in the air and the two begin singing. They aren't horrible, but also not great. But at least the way they are shaking their asses onstage is entertaining. I laugh lightly and keep my eyes on the stage.

"You make it home okay last night?" Jonas's voice breaks my trance on the singing duo. And when I peer over at him to speak, guilt riddles me at the concern stretched over his face. Normal me would have let him know I made it home safely. Normal me was absent last night.

Since the day Jonas and I met, there has always been an easy way about us. Jonas is a great guy. Genuine and thoughtful and kindhearted. He knows how to have fun and make people laugh. And there is no denying I like him. But nothing more could ever happen between us. It wouldn't be fair to him if I couldn't be all in. That and his former relationship statuses.

"Yeah," I mumble. "Gavin drove me home in my car."

He nods, slow and steady, as his eyes stay fixed on his plate. Although his head is down, I notice the twitches in his expression. The flickers of emotion he doesn't want on display. And it's a stab to the heart that he doesn't want me to know what he feels or thinks.

Please look at me. Don't shut me out. That is what I *want* to say to him, but I stop myself. I don't want to send him mixed messages. Say words that mean one thing but could be interpreted in some misconstrued way.

Jonas and I have been friends for years now. I don't have many male friends or acquaintances—not on purpose—and I can't imagine having a better guy friend than him. Things with Jonas… nothing is complicated or artificial. What you see is what you get. And that is not a bad thing. I never have to question our friendship or who he is or what his motives are.

He is sweet and funny and would go out of his way to help a stranger. Having him in my company has never been weird. And although I know things have shifted a little between us, he would do anything for me. As I would for him. Like a true friend.

"Can I ask you something?" Jonas asks. Erin and Shelly sit across from us, chatting separately.

"You know you can," I tell him. Because it's true. I don't hide who I am from people I trust.

"What's going on with you and Gavin?" His face serious. More serious than I have seen it over the years.

"Not sure what you mean. He's the model I'm shooting right now."

In actuality, I know exactly what he means. Where his question is directed. He wants to know the history between us, and how that affects things now. I have no intention of lying to Jonas, but I don't want to spew word vomit and overshare information he doesn't want to hear. There is no need to dredge up things better left behind.

He cocks his head and studies my face a moment. "You know that's not what I mean. There's something else going on between the two of you. Am I right?"

I have no clue. God, I wish I knew the answer. The seesaw of emotions makes me nauseous. "Maybe. But I don't know," I say with a shrug.

His bluish-hazel eyes bore into mine as he tries to read the words left unsaid. Under the table, his knee brushes against my leg and I close my eyes as the contact sends a rush of jitters through my chest. There is no use in denying my attraction to Jonas. After all, he is easy on the eyes and looks at me as if no other woman walks the earth.

What woman doesn't want a man like that? Someone who only sees her.

The music fades into the background as his knee stays pressed against me. My eyes remain closed and my food forgotten. His weight shifts against me, his knee sliding higher up the outside of my thigh as I feel him lean into me. My breathing picks up as his rough stubble grazes against my cheek. *What is he doing?* I might just have a heart attack in the middle of the bar.

His breath is hot on my ear and I stop breathing altogether. "I hope not," he whispers. "Because that wouldn't bode well for me." And then he kisses me below the ear, trailing two more below it before pulling away.

Damnit. I am so royally fucked.

My heart hammers against my rib cage while my lungs try to remember how to work. His knee slides back to where it was moments earlier, but still touches me. The three spots where his lips touched my skin singe and sting, as if branding me with his essence.

The idea of opening my eyes scares the hell out of me. I'm scared of what I will see and feel and possibly realize. The overwhelming sensation has crept into my veins many times, but I purposely shove it down. Emotions and thoughts that tell me it is okay to like Jonas more than a friend. That it's okay to want someone other than the boy—now man—who holds my heart prisoner.

God, what do Shelly and Erin think of me right now? As I sit on this stool and fight the urge to kiss a man I have thought about kissing countless times, but stopped myself because my heart steps up to the plate.

I take a deep breath and harness every ounce of bravery inside me as I open my eyes. Jonas's link to mine immediately. Something different resides within them, though. Fire. Passion. Desires he has kept smoldering for years. Has all this come to life because Gavin is here? Is he finally acting on how he feels for me because he fears his chances are fading?

Or has jealousy brought them to the forefront? I don't want jealousy to be the reason he chooses to make a move. Jealousy isn't the right reason to tell someone you care for them.

Looking across the table, I realize Erin and Shelly are absent. "Where are…" I trail off.

"They went to the bathroom before stepping outside to make a call," he informs me.

"Together?" I ask, the absurdity of it layering my tone.

"I guess so. They got up at the same time and went the same way." His eyes never leave me. "Does that bother you? That they left us alone."

My eyes dart between his and I suddenly see him a little different than I did ten minutes ago. "No. Don't be silly. Of course it doesn't bother me." I snatch an onion ring to occupy my mouth before I ramble any further.

"Good." His arm inches closer to me and his warm hand rests atop my bopping knee. "Because I'd hate to think you're nervous to be around me now."

It is not that I'm nervous per se to be around Jonas. More like I don't want history repeating itself. The last guy I loved—who had also been my best friend beforehand—moved across the country. Granted, it wasn't his choice to do so, but he made zero effort to return. I put in all the effort and he just didn't. The only reason Gavin is here now is because his work brought him here. Not me.

If this shoot hadn't come up, would he have returned?

I have asked myself this question too many times this week. Have questioned if he ever had intentions of returning. Even if I ask Gavin, would he tell me the truth? Or only what I want to hear? Would he sugarcoat the reason it took him more than a decade to come back here? To me. If he is doing so well in his career, if he still loves me the way he claims, why didn't he return sooner? This whole situation frustrates me on so many levels. I don't know which way is up anymore.

God, it feels as if I'm in the middle of an epic battle. The battle for my affection. And somehow, I became the prize. Against my own volition. What if I want things to stay how they are? What if I don't want a relationship— other than friendship—with either one of them? Do I get a say in the matter? Of all the people in this situation, I should get the biggest say in the outcome. My heart is the one on the line, after all.

"I'm not nervous to be around you," I say after a long stretch of silence. "More worried, I guess."

"Worried?" He is quick to ask.

"Yes. I don't want things to change. And whether intentional or not, relationships change the dynamic between people and friendships. This" —I point between the two of us— "is perfect right now. What if us being more than what we are changes that? I can't lose you as a friend, Jonas. It would crush me."

Jonas's fingers trace small circles above my knee, the gentle motion is soothing and worrisome. I have always enjoyed Jonas's company. Always smiled and laughed and had a good time when we were together.

A time here and there, I thought maybe he wanted more than friendship, but he never made a move or asked me on a date. So I brushed it off and assumed I read him wrong.

Ninety-nine percent of our outings include Shelly and/or Erin. It isn't me not wanting to spend individual time with him. More like the thought never occurred to me for us to hang out alone. Jonas is my friend, and I usually do friend stuff in group settings. Things have always been that way. And only occasionally veer off.

"Believe me, I know exactly where you're coming from. That's the reason I've never said anything. Never put myself out there to you. Because I'd be broken without you," he confesses then pauses, taking a breath before locking eyes with me. "But now… it seems like if I wait to tell you how I feel, I'll miss the opportunity. Or I could lose you. He's had your heart once before. If he's lucky enough to have it again, I…"

He doesn't finish his thought as he drops his chin, but I know what he would have said. *I wouldn't stand a chance.* Is he right? If Gavin somehow won my heart again, would I cave and be with him? Part of me instantly says yes—the part that has longed for him for years. Another part of me says no—that being the logical, rational side. The side that reminds me of the painful days, the loneliness and the heartache from before. All the tears and cold nights and nightmares.

I lay my hand over Jonas's and his eyes jerk up to

meet mine. "I know," I tell him. "But no matter what, you'll always be a part of me."

Seconds later, Shelly and Erin plop back on their stools and look over at the woman singing karaoke. My thoughts run on high speed, and I have no clue what song is playing, nor do I care. All I know is, below the wooden grain of this tall tabletop, Jonas hasn't removed his hand, and neither have I.

Fifteen years ago

ONE MORE HOUR and Thanksgiving break starts. Nine glorious days of not getting up before the sun. Of sleeping in and zero required reading or assignments. But those aren't the best parts of time off school. Not by a long shot.

What I'm really over the moon about is having uninterrupted time with Cora.

Sure, I see her throughout the week at school. And sporadically we see each other on the weekend to "study." But we are never really alone. When we are "studying," it is in her living room or mine, our parents not far away. One of us on the couch, the other between their legs on the floor.

On occasion, I catch myself playing with a strand of her hair while she sits in front of me, arms warm against the inside of my calves. Or I lean into her legs when I'm cross-legged on the floor. She never brushes me off or acts as if the gesture makes her uncomfortable. And every once in a while, the light brushing of her fingertips draws on the skin of my neck. When she does this, I have to remember how to breathe. How to think.

We have preplanned a couple days of Thanksgiving break. Meeting with friends, hanging out and playing Putt-Putt or bowling. But I hope she will want to spend more time together, just the pair of us. Within a week of school starting, she easily slipped into friend—if not best friend—territory. A week after that, I craved to see her as much as possible and had an inkling she would always be more. At least to me. And I hope she reciprocates.

The bell rings and cheers can be heard throughout the school. Cheers of a week of freedom and sleep and no schedule. Cheers to less supervision and good times with friends. Closing my textbook, I stuff it and my notebook into my backpack. I slide out of my seat with a smile plastered on my face and head out the door. This week will be perfect.

Through the dark lenses on my sunglasses, I stare out at the water and watch Cora as she splashes Shelly in the shallows. Although it is late November, the sun beats down mild temperatures ranging from the low eighties to the high seventies in this part of Florida. The Gulf is still warm, but will cool in the next couple of weeks.

Micah, Shelly's older brother and my best friend for the last few years, sits next to me and doesn't hide the fact he ogles women ten-plus years his senior. But I'm cool with him being distracted. It disguises the fact I can't seem to remove my eyes from Cora's creamy white skin. The pallor similar to the snow I saw last winter when my parents took us on a road trip during winter break.

Hair black as coal, skin white as cotton, lips red as fresh cherries. Her smile bright as the sun on a summer day and her laugh a sound that sings to my heartstrings the moment I hear it.

Everything about her stunning. Spellbinding. Hypnotizing.

It's not until Micah backhands my bicep that I realize he has been talking to me and I have no clue what he said. "Sorry, man. What?" And I will my eyes to leave Cora to look over at Micah.

"I said we picked the perfect day to come out here. Lots of oil-slicked beauties out today," he states, brows waggling. Today is one of those days when Micah behaves like the typical horny teenage boy. Both annoying and not. But he is my best friend and I tolerate his ways.

There is only one person I have an interest in looking at, but for the sake of not being razzed, I nod and add, "Definitely a perfect day." I leave my response generic, hoping he won't press further.

But Micah isn't the type of guy to leave things unsaid. I have only known him a short time, but it hasn't taken long to learn how outgoing he is. "Anyone catching your eye? You've been a little zoned out."

Only one person has caught my eye, but I have no intention of divulging this tidbit. Not now. "No one in particular. You?"

"There's a trio of blondes at three o'clock I've been watching for a few. Think I might go say hello. You want to go with?"

"Nah. Think I'll cool off in the water for a bit."

I would rather be inches away from the magnetic girl sporting a black two-piece with curves in all the right places.

Micah rises from the blanket, brushes sand off his legs and board shorts, and straightens his spine. I'm half tempted to tell him it doesn't matter if you have sand on you, dipshit, you're at the beach. We are surrounded by sand. But I opt to refrain from jabbing him.

In a few quick strides, he walks away from me and makes a beeline for the females who I hope will occupy his time a while. After I'm certain he is not turning back,

I scoot to the edge of the blanket and stare out at the water a moment. Cora and Shelly tread water just deep enough to reach the edge of their shoulders. They talk about something, Shelly's hand animating above the water every five seconds. Cora watches her studiously behind the dark tint of her sunglasses and smiles here and there.

Deep breath in, I stand from our reserved spot on the beach and trek fifty feet toward the water's edge. The small waves break over my shins as I shuffle into the water. Once I stand waist deep in the salty surf, I sink in the water, and wet my hair before swimming to Cora and Shelly.

As I approach them, I hear them talking about seeing a movie later. Intrigued, I wonder if I will be invited to said movie. Who cares what plays on the screen, I would love to just sit beside Cora for two hours in the dim-lit theater. Would I even be able to focus on the movie? Probably not.

"Hey," Cora says, breathless. I tread water on her right until I realize I can reach the sand below, planting my feet but keeping my body the same height as the two of them. "Tired of tanning yourself." A teasing smile lights her face.

"Ha-ha. Micah walked off to hit on some chicks and I was getting toasty on the blanket. Thought I'd see what you two were up to."

"We were just talking about seeing a movie later,"

Shelly chimes in. "Not sure what's playing, but we could pick whatever. Usually, there's always something good at the theater around the holidays."

"I'm in, if that's okay with you guys," I tell them both.

"Cool," Shelly pants, her body winded from treading water so long. "I'm gonna head back to the blanket, tan for a little, and see if anyone else wants to join us."

Before either of us says another word, Shelly swims to shore and leaves me alone with Cora. Exactly what I was hoping for.

In the anonymity of the water, my hands itch to reach forward and grab hold of her waist. I stare at her dark lenses through mine, neither of us uttering a word. We have never needed to fill time with meaningless conversation. By some unknown universal connection, we can read each other without ever speaking a word.

As if she hears my thoughts, as if she knows the urge building inside me, she swims closer and stops inches from my frame. The water surrounding me ebbs and flows with her arm and leg movements as she continues to tread. I stop fighting my instinct. Stop resisting what is in front of me.

The moment my hands grasp the curves of her waist, her arms and legs still. To anyone looking from the shore, nothing has changed except for her lack of distance. Our bodies hidden in the wide open. It is exhilarating. Not that I care if anyone sees us together. If anything, it would be heaven to tell the world my feelings for Cora. Feelings that have been growing stronger by the minute.

One hand holds her steady while the other begins to trace lines along the side of her torso. Up and down. Bikini top to bikini bottom. Her lips part just enough to see past the bold red rouge.

Under the water, her chest expands and contracts under my touch. She doesn't stop me, but I have to know if she is okay with me touching her like this. As much as it would devastate me to hear her say no, I would never press her for something she had no desire to pursue. I don't want to ruin what we have.

Leaning forward, my face an inch or two from hers, I whisper, "Is this okay?"

Her breath hitches, and I wonder if her eyes are closed behind her heavy-tinted lenses. She nods, her voice breathy when she speaks. "Yes."

Her fingertips brush over my chest, startling me. "Sorry," I mutter. "Just unexpected."

She doesn't say anything in response, her fingers exploring my chest as we bob in the water. Minutes pass, the sounds of other beachgoers fade away. All that exists is her and me and our bodies growing closer and closer as we explore each other's skin.

My eyes drop from her frames, focusing on her lips and wondering what it would be like to kiss her. I have dreamed of kissing a few girls before, but that is all. Just dreams. But I think if I kiss Cora, I will never want to kiss another person in my life. My eyes pop back up to hers, wishing I could see her bold green irises. See what she is thinking. What she is feeling. If they hold the same questions or possibility mine do.

Without thinking, I close the last inches between us. My head tilting, lips hovering breathless above hers, waiting to see if she backs away. When she doesn't draw back, I take the gesture as invitation and seal my lips to hers.

Warm, soft lips press against mine, her hands breaching the water's surface and wrapping around my neck. I pull her impossibly closer to me, swiping the tip of my tongue over her lips and relishing in the sensation when she parts them and lets me in.

Her mouth is sweet and hungry on mine. And when a small whimper echoes in her chest, I am a goner. My hands roam her body under the security blanket of the water, kneading and caressing her hips. We stay like this, the measure of time nonexistent.

But when I feel her legs wrap around my waist, her strength locking us together at the hips, I break my mouth from hers, gasping. At this rate, things will progress much quicker than either of us is prepared to handle. In public, no less.

"Why'd you stop?" she asks, confusion lacing her voice.

"Because we have forever. And I don't want to rush anything with you."

She leans into me, pressing a sweet, brief kiss to my lips. "I like the sound of that."

TWENTY-ONE

GAVIN

Present

"I DON'T UNDERSTAND the issue, man," Micah harps from the driver's seat. "I may not grasp what's going on between the two of you. Honestly, I never have. But you got to do what's best for you."

Why is it so hard to talk about women and relationships with guy friends? Unless they are in a relationship, everything comes out piggish.

Over the years, I've had several female friends. One of my best friends in Cali is female. We could talk about anything. Have in-depth conversations, no matter the topic, and come out feeling resolute. None of that is happening right now. Maybe because Micah has never been in my position. Never felt torn or anguished or helpless because of someone else.

"That's the problem. I'm not sure I know what's best for me anymore," I groan. "Before my mom took the promotion and moved us across the country, I had everything mapped out. Things changed days after we landed in California. Not only was my life turned upside down, everything I thought I'd have was ripped away from me." I pause, taking a swig of water before continuing. "Over the last decade-plus, she's always been the one thing I held on to. Even if I was the only one who knew. And now…"

Music blares from the speakers, masking the silence between us. Micah has no comprehension of what I am going through. My inner turmoil. A waging war roaring inside me. One side says I should head back to California when this shoot ends, leave her behind and allow her to resume the life she has built without me. The other side screams at me to return to California, sell my shit, strategize my future gigs and return to Cora's side. Sensible versus senseless.

The decision is one only I can make, but I was hoping for some form of support. Maybe some strong words of advice. Or just some *if I were in your shoes* talk. And unfortunately for me, Micah is no help whatsoever.

"And now, someone else is trying to step up to the plate," Micah states over the music. He states the obvious and my blood runs cold. I shiver at the thought of Cora being with someone. Someone who isn't me. Yes, I am a selfish ass for even thinking that way. But I left my heart with her all those years ago. I refuse to let an outsider stomp his steel-toes on it and whisk away my girl.

He steers the car into a parking lot, finding a spot amongst the crowd. We step out of the car and head for the entrance. Music blares loud and obnoxious every time the doors swing open. As we climb the few steps, I slap the back of his shoulder. "Thanks for bringing me out tonight. And thanks for listening."

"I'd be a dick if I didn't."

The whole situation with me and Cora is the furthest thing from what Micah wants to discuss, but he has always been a good friend. If anything, he probably just wants us to get things figured out—whichever way it turns out—and be done with all this back and forth shit.

We walk through the doors and the music hits me like a wall. Micah gestures to the bar when he steps up to the hostess stand and she signals us to head over. Both of us park on a stool and order a beer when the bartender comes over. After she deposits them in front of us, we each take a sip before sparking more conversation.

Micah and I catch up on life, avoiding all subject matter that could lead to Cora. He relays how the night-club he manages is going. I suggest he brings me out there before I leave. He talks about an older woman, Rochelle, he dated for a little over a year. How serious his and Rochelle's relationship was until he found her fucking another guy. A guy ten years younger than

Micah, and twenty-three years younger than Rochelle. Many heated words were exchanged between the two of them, but Micah said he would never be able to trust her again.

Since the relationship with Rochelle, Micah hasn't committed to anyone. He no longer sees the value in devoting yourself to one person. In his words, "setting yourself up for pain and heartbreak." Now, over the last year since they broke up, he is a proud manwhore. And when he tells me this, a pang of guilt hits me over the manwhore moments I have had myself.

Because over the last thirteen years, I have never wanted a relationship with anyone other than Cora. Although, I have gone on dates. Fucked a sea of women. Never once feeling guilt over suppressing the loneliness inside me. But now that I am back here. Now that I am within proximity of her. Everything is changing.

Micah prattles on about themed nights they do at the club, and I zone out while my eyes wander around the bar. The place is packed, which isn't abnormal for a Friday night anywhere. Bodies dancing on a makeshift dance floor. Tall tabletops littered with brown bottles, fried foods, and pint glassware. Horrible, screechy voices up on an eight-by-eight stage attempting to sing lyrics on a prompter. No matter where you are in the States, bars are bars. The only thing different is the accents and clothing.

As I make a final visual circuit of the bar, I freeze when I hit a tabletop close to the corner of the room.

Rage gushes in my bloodstream. My heart bashing against my ribcage like a boxer to a punching bag. Everything inside me molten lava and I am ready to beat the shit out of someone. Specifically, the brown-haired motherfucker touching my girl.

I kick back the stool, hitting the person behind me and causing Micah's head to swing my way. "Dude, you okay?" he asks.

My eyes fix across the room, hands balled into fists at my sides, breath heaving in my chest. Micah touches my arm and I flinch at the contact. When I don't answer him, he follows my line of sight and mutters *fuck me* under his breath.

"Let's just go, man. They're friends."

I hear his words, but can't take my eyes off *his* hand on *her* thigh. *Friends, my ass.* They may be *friends*, but he definitely wants to be more than her friend. And I am not having it.

Yanking my wallet out, I drop a twenty on the bar and storm off, half my beer forgotten. As I weave my way through the crowded bar, I hear Micah yelling for me, telling me to just leave it alone. But there is no chance in hell I am walking out of here and ignoring the two of them together. No fucking way.

I am ten feet and three bodies away from them when Cora looks up, her eyes going wide and her body scooting off the stool. She reaches me before I can get close enough to the table. Close enough to beat the shit out of this guy.

"Gavin!" she yells at me over the music. My eyes lock on his, and the self-assured smile he throws at me has me trying to push Cora aside. But her hand comes to my face and instantly stops me. "Gavin!" she yells again. This time I look down at her, noticing the fear in her soft green eyes.

We stare at each other a minute, her eyes trying to tell me that everything is not as it appears. I want to believe her. God, how I want to believe her. I have no reason to doubt her or her truths. But my insecurities sit on my shoulder, mocking me and whispering falsehoods into my ear. Telling me I will never have her again. Reminding me how I lost her once and how I will lose her again.

"It's not what you think," she whispers, and I have to read her lips over the noise.

"And what was I thinking?" I prompt.

"That we're on a date. That we're more than friends." Her voice grows loud enough to break the volume barrier, but not loud enough for others to hear us.

"His hand looked quite cozy on your thigh. For someone who's *just a friend,*" I sneer.

Her hand runs down my chest and squeezes my hand. "Come outside with me." And then she pushes past me, towing me out of the bar and away from *him.*

We weave through the crowd, exit the front and continue walking until she stops us beside her car in the back of the lot. When she spins around, she drops my hand and hits me with years of anger and frustration.

"What the hell, Gavin!"

"Sorry I interrupted your date with mister auto shop," I jab, laying the sarcasm on thick. "I thought you two were just friends. Looks like he seems to think otherwise. Maybe I should go back inside and reiterate the definition for him."

"First of all" —she points her finger in my face— "you have no say in regards to who I date and who I don't. Second, why do you suddenly think you're all high and mighty? What… you stroll back into town and think the whole place stopped existing when you left. That everything is exactly as it was when you left. Newsflash, asshole. Nothing is how you left it. Nothing."

"I can see that," I seethe, stepping closer into her space. "If it was how I left it, this conversation wouldn't ever happen. We'd be…" I bite my tongue.

"What? What exactly would we be doing, Gavin?"

God, she is gorgeous when she gets angry. Dangerously so. And before I can form a rational response in my head, I reach for her face and drag her into me, crushing my lips to hers. Her hands shove and beat against my chest, her lips trying to pull away. But I strengthen my grip and get lost in the feel of her. The warmth. Her taste.

In two breaths, her will caves and she melts into me.

Her hands fist my shirt as she kisses me with a fervor I have never known. I wrap one arm around her waist while the other hand skims up her back and gets lost in the length of her strands.

The kiss is packed with anger and frustration, fear and worry, happiness and pain. But most of all, it shares the depth of our deprivation. How neither of us has been complete since the day my mother put me on a plane and flew me thousands of miles away. How we have gone about life, but had forgotten what it was like to live.

She breaks the kiss, gasping for air as she tries to come back down to earth. When both of our bodies have calmed, she peeks up at me. "Gavin…" My name a blessing and a curse on her tongue. "Please. Please don't hurt me again. I can't…" she pleads. Begs me not to put her through the heartache she suffered thirteen years ago.

I yank her impossibly close to my chest, my arms cocooning her frail frame. "Shh. I know, baby. I know." The ease with which the term of endearment slips out isn't lost on me. It also doesn't appear to bother Cora. We stand like this—her clutching me and me pressing her to my chest, rocking her—for minutes, maybe hours. Letting her go isn't an option I am comfortable with, so I hold her and wait for her to break the connection. Praying she never will.

"Can we go somewhere to talk? I really don't want to stand in this parking lot all night," she whispers.

"Yeah. Wherever you want to go, baby."

Somehow, we land on the beach. Of all the places we could have gone, not quite sure why she picked the beach. The park across the street from her house is more her style. But maybe she chose the beach because it is mine. Or maybe she chose the beach because that is where everything evolved for us. Where everything went from friends to something words can't describe.

Either way, she is with me now and it is the only thing I focus on.

When we arrive at the beach, she pays a meter and we stroll north. After separating from the busier section of the beach, everything around us grows quieter and calmer. The only sounds are the crunch of sand under our shoes and the choppy water breaking on the shore. The air thick with humidity and salty on our skin. This part of the beach darker with the lack of businesses to illuminate it. A few residents out for a late-night walk.

Her hand presses softly against mine as she stops us from walking any further in the soft sand. Plopping down, our fingers still woven together, we sit on the beach and face the darkness of the Gulf. Neither of us says a word. We simply sit in silence and lean into each other for a while. Her ink-black hair whips across her face and mine.

The ease I have with Cora has never been replicated with any other person. Over the years, I tried dating. Tried putting myself out there and moving on, certain Cora was doing the same. And over time, I learned I would never find someone else who I'd want to be in a long-term relationship with. So, I shifted my ways. Became the polar opposite of how everyone knew me. Morphed into a slut. Because slutting around was easier than finding someone else and losing the one person you really wanted all along.

Because regardless of how things go between us now, Cora is it for me. The one soul on this planet, packed with eight billion others, meant for me. I have known it since the first day I saw her in high school, when she bolted into homeroom out of breath, making me out of breath. Confirmed it when we kissed for the first time, a beach not many miles from this one, and my soul sighed while my heart soared. I will never experience that with another person.

Nor do I want to.

"Gavin," she whispers into the darkness, breaking me from my introspection.

I turn and kiss her temple. "What, baby?"

She rests her chin on my shoulder, the waning moonlight illuminating her enough to where I can make out the soft lines and strong features of her face. Eyes a muted green in the shadows. Skin seemingly paler. Lips red and full and inviting. "How can this possibly work?" Her question weighs heavy and is full of doubt.

How can I reassure her everything will work out? That I have the capability to move closer to her. How I don't have to be located on the other side of the country to work. I know she should know this, with what she does for work. But there is only one way she will believe it all. Proof. And I have to give it to her.

My eyes hone in on hers. "I want to move back. The sooner, the better," I admit.

She straightens her back, stiffening at my admission. A thick strand of her ebony hair whips across her face, hiding her eyes from me. She doesn't move to swipe the hairs aside, and I force myself to keep my hands rooted in place, as challenging as it is. Minutes pass, the wind shifts and brushes the hair away. As desperate as she is to school her expressions, I read her like a book. Always have.

Curiosity. Speculation. Doubt. Fear. Elation. It is all written there in an ink only my eyes see.

I grab hold of the elation and press it close to my chest. Of all the emotions swirling in her eyes, it is the one that raises my hope for us. That we can find our way back to each other.

"But how?" Her question as wispy as the wind.

Cupping her left cheek, I brush my thumb over her

plump lower lip. *God, I want to kiss her again.* But I must wait. Wait until she is certain that I am still what she wants. As much as it guts me to think of her with another guy, it isn't right of me to assume she will come back to me as easily. I hurt her.

"Baby, I can live anywhere and do my job. With what you do, you have to know this."

"But what about your life out there? Your parents? How can I ask you to leave everything you've built out there? It isn't fair for me to do that."

Her question about my parents strikes a chord in my chest. I'm not ready to update her on what has happened in that part of my life. Not until I know she is open to exploring *us* again. "You don't need to worry about that. Since the day we set foot in California, my mom has heard nothing except my orchestrated plans to leave. And you may believe it isn't fair for you to ask me to come back here. Back to you." I reach forward and press my palm against her sternum. "But this is where I belong. This is where I have always belonged. You are all that matters. All that has ever mattered."

She sucks in a breath as her eyes pool with unshed tears. In the shadowed night of the beach, everything is heightened and intensified. As if being in the darkness provides a blanket of security and you feel safe enough to expose your heart. There is something to be said about the darkness and its allure. Not just the darkness of night, but the yin in all things. That is what she is... my yin. The strong, feminine cosmic force who took hold of my heart and molded it with hers. Without her, I am a pointless yang. No balance, no life, no love.

Soft, thin fingers rest atop mine, encompassing my hand in the warmth of her skin. Below my palm, her heart beats wildly. Irrationally. While her heart tells me tales of excitement and joy, her eyes shed tears of insecurity and apprehension. Both of which I understand.

But a glint of something else resides there. Hope. A belief there is truth behind my words. That I am not just saying these things to taunt or mislead her. That there is an actual chance for us to rekindle something that never should have been diffused in the first place. A new opportunity to share the undeniable magnetism we have always had for each other. Hope for a new version of us. A better version.

"How?" The single word a question that rests heavy on her lips.

"I've been talking about moving back home for years. And now that my career has a better base, I can live anywhere. I don't have to be in the thick of Hollywood for people to find me. It was different in the beginning. Being out there helped get my foot in the door. Got me in front of the right people. But now... now I can be wherever. Alyson deals with all the contractual and legal aspects. She lets me know when someone is interested in hiring me. Sure, me living out there makes life easier for her. But she can still be my agent no matter where I am. Technology allows people to be on opposite sides of the world and still work together."

Beside me, Cora's body softens and relaxes into my side once more. And it feels so fucking good to have her body pressed against mine. Her warmth and energy radiating into me. Soothing me. Revitalizing me. Like being home again. She rests her head on my shoulder and I rest mine on hers, closing my eyes and breathing in this moment.

Waves crash along the shoreline, cars rev and honk in the distance, wind whips our hair and I can't tell where hers stops and mine begins. But neither of us moves. Both of us in a strange limbo of emotions and confessions. Our hearts thrown on the line, praying to not suffer the same pain as before. Promises exposed and hanging on the line as we breathe the same air for the first time in years.

But one truth holds absolute. I could sit with her on this beach for hours, not a soul around us, and feel nothing except bliss for the rest of my days. Everything about this moment is perfect. Everything about this moment is us.

Time evades us and I get lost in thoughts of what could be, causing me to almost miss when she speaks again.

"When?"

I am half tempted to tease her regarding the singular

worded questions, but I bite my tongue. Now isn't the time to tease and play.

"When the shoot ends, I'll obviously need to go back. Alyson set up another shoot for me, but it should only be a day or two. And even though I don't have to do it in person, I need to go talk with my mom. Tell her I plan to move back as soon as possible. She is the only person, besides Alyson, who needs to know."

She lifts her head, stopping me. "What about your dad?" she asks, confused at why I only mentioned my mom.

I didn't want tonight to be when I brought this to light, but it looks as though I will have to tell her now. I take a deep breath and hold her gaze. The only set of eyes to ever provide me solace. "My dad passed away a couple years ago. Heart attack."

Instantly, her arms pull me into an embrace, lips at my ears softly whispering through light sobs. "Gavin, I'm so sorry. I didn't know."

Instinctively, my arms curl around her frame and I bring her closer to me. Within seconds, her legs straddle my lap and lock together at my backside. Yin and Yang. She weeps for me and my family. And I allow myself this moment to be raw, shedding tears for a man who was my role model for so many years. A man I have grieved for and thought I would eventually find peace after his passing. Until now. Sharing this with Cora makes the loss of him more potent and noteworthy. More real and closer to my heart.

Part of me forgot my mom and I weren't the only people to lose him. When Cora and I started dating, my parents became hers too. After so many years apart, it never dawned on me to let her know sooner of his passing. Especially since we hadn't spoken for more than a decade.

When the tears quiet, she doesn't remove herself from our embrace. As if she knows the power it holds. As if she isn't ready to let it float off with the tide.

"Thank you," I whisper into her hair, my hands stroking lazy trails up and down her back.

"For what?" she asks, head tucked in the crook of my neck.

"For saying the right words. And just being you. Everyone I've told says or shows me pity. Or walks on eggshells when we're in the same room. As if I'm this fragile creature who will crumple. So, thank you. You've always known how to say just enough to convey the right thing."

I press a kiss to her temple and her arms and legs squeeze me tighter. We sit like this a little while longer before I make a suggestion to check the time. She pulls her phone from her back pocket, lighting the screen and mutters *shit*.

"Must be late," I assume. We have been here a while.

Felt like hours. But when emotions are heightened, time has a tendency to not measure the same way clocks do.

"Almost two. We should go. We have to be at Honeymoon Island by ten. Somewhere in there, both of us need to sleep and eat and whatever else."

I laugh at her slight state of panic. "It'll be fine." I stand us up, her legs tightening around my waist, arms circling my neck. "Let me walk you back to your car."

After a few strides, she unhooks her ankles and drops her feet to the sand. Once she is upright, I weave my fingers with hers and we trudge through the powdery sand and back to her car. Every six or seven steps, I glance down at her and happiness floods my heart. Warmth and love and everything right in the world.

Fuck, I have missed her.

We reach her car ten minutes later. She offers to drive me the quarter mile back to my hotel, but I decline, wanting to walk back and reminisce over tonight. She slips into the driver's seat, starts the car and rolls down the front windows. Her hair whips across her face and steals my view of her perfect, soft green irises.

Bending down, I tuck the strands behind her ear and relish the way she leans into my touch. "I'll see you in the morning." *Fuck, I want to kiss her again.* My thumb brushes over her lower lip and she shudders, eyes slipping shut. How easy would it be to kiss her right now? But I don't. I won't. From now on, she needs to lead me. She needs to let me know she wants this as much as I do.

I cannot be the only one putting myself out there. The only one pressing for this. For us.

When her eyes open, they smolder and I feel it deep in my groin. "See you soon," she mumbles, releasing a deep breath.

I step back from the window, internally cursing myself for not taking what I want. But I know I am doing the right thing. All good things come to those who wait. Right? She pulls out of the parking space, gives me a brief wave and drives down the road. Taking a chunk of me with her into the night.

Fourteen years ago

THANK God it is the last day of school. I have never really been one to not like school, in fact I have always been eager to be there. But I am counting down the minutes, psyched to have the summer off and spending more time with Gavin. This school year is one to go down as a year worth remembering. So much has happened, and it is unimaginable that I am dating my best friend.

Weekdays seem to snail along, with the exception of when Gavin and I are together. Most weeknights we study together. And by study, I mean finish homework between make-out sessions. Not that I have another person to compare it to, but Gavin really knows how to kiss a girl senseless. It is ironic we are both each other's firsts. First real relationship. First kiss. Those two kisses before Gavin don't count since neither guy knew what they were doing either.

Oftentimes, I wonder what other firsts we will share. Perhaps we will be the first people, besides our family, we say *I love you* to. Just thinking about him makes me want to scream it to the world. Let everyone know he belongs to me. And I belong to him. But I want to wait for the perfect time. To say the words to him when everything feels perfect.

Another first that has crossed my mind is sex. I know neither of us is quite ready yet.

We have been friends since the beginning of the school year, which turned into best friends within weeks. But we have only been girlfriend and boyfriend for six and a half months. Plus, we are only fifteen. Isn't sex something you wait to do when you are closer to adulthood? At least that is what all the adults tell you. But who knows when it's actually okay.

Any day now, it wouldn't surprise me if Mom and Dad have "the talk" with me. The talk is just a load of crap they tell you so you will stay focused on whatever it is they want you to focus on. Parents think having sex equals not doing anything else in life. I wonder if my parents dreaded the infamous talk. By now, everyone the same age as me has had at least one or two sex-ed classes —we aren't stupid. And we all have access to the internet.

But now... as I sit here in my English honors class,

I'm not focused on the teacher—who yammers on about what books we should be reading over summer break. Nope. Instead, my mind swims with thoughts of me and Gavin and summer break and making out and sex. Anyone glancing my way would certainly notice the flush spreading along my face and neck.

From head to toe, I am hot. And it has nothing to do with the stifling outdoor temperatures.

Sex isn't a topic either of us has broached while together. But the thought has probably crossed his mind if it has crossed mine. How could it not? Don't guys think about sex more often than girls? That is what everyone says. Is he sitting in class right now thinking about it? Probably not. Geometry and sex aren't two subjects that pair well. Then again, I'm ignoring everything my teacher says and thinking about it. What's to say Gavin isn't doing the same. If I think about sex every other minute of the day, is Gavin constantly thinking about it?

Sex, sex, sex.

I shake my head, trying to clear my thoughts and catch Ms. Winters' final thoughts on summer reading. "Everyone, be sure to pick up a copy of the summer reading list from my desk before you go," she says a minute before the bell rings. "The sheet also has a few minor assignments you can earn extra credit on from your sophomore English teacher when school resumes." Thank God everything she just told us is on paper.

The bell buzzes for the final time of my freshman year and cheers erupt from every classroom in the quad. Twenty-three of us rise from our desks, gather our belongings and head for the door. I grab a copy of the printout and wish Ms. Winters a happy summer break. She gives me a brief smile on my way to the door and returns the sentiment.

When I step out into the summer sun, I take a deep breath and tilt my chin to the sky, closing my eyes. I stand there a moment, hundreds of bodies moving around me like the running of the bulls. Summer fever is in the air and everyone is excited to not be here for months. Me included.

Strong, warm arms circle around my waist, tugging me back until I make contact with the body behind me. *Gavin.* I would know him anywhere. Even if I couldn't see him, I would know he was there. That is just the connection we have with each other. An inexplicable bond fusing us together. Like a form of symbiosis.

I twist in his arms and turn enough to see his radiant smile in the sunlight. "Hey," I say.

He kisses me sweetly on the lips before responding. "Hey. You ready to get out of here?"

"Definitely. Want to grab something to eat? I think a bunch of people are headed to the sub shop."

"Yeah. Micah and Shelly are going. He said he'd give us a ride after if we went," Gavin states.

"Cool. Anything you want to do after?"

"I thought maybe we could hang and watch your favorite movies on repeat."

Like a five-year-old, I start jumping up and down like a fool. "Seriously?!" I plant a quick kiss on his lips. "You really are the best boyfriend ever."

His returning smile and hug tells me he knows.

We are curled up on the couch, my back to Gavin's front, as *Lord of the Rings* plays on the television. We have just reached the part where Arwen is trying to help save Frodo's life because he had the ring on too long. Gavin stretches behind me, adjusting his arm as we spoon in the dim living room of my house.

His finger slowly skims up and down the side of my torso, repeating the circuit over and over. Since we started dating, he has touched me like this countless times. The soft strokes are sweet and soothing and stir flutters in my chest. But today, his touch feels different. My skin hotter. My body needier. Breath heavier. Heart more anxious. Only I'm not sure if it is just me feeling it.

God, I hope it isn't just me feeling it.

My parents won't be home from work for at least another two hours. And the realization of this tidbit causes perspiration to break free across my skin. My heart thump, thump, thumps louder in my chest. A tight pinch in my lungs as I try to breathe normal and not start panting. His fingers light a frenzy under my skin everywhere he touches.

When his fingers graze over the curve of my hip, my eyes roll back and I close my lids. A deep breath later and I roll over to face him. Once I resituate, his fingers continue their slow, sensual tease of my opposite side. I study his face, the light from the screen dimming and brightening with the scene and hiding his face every few seconds.

"You don't want to watch the movie?" he asks, confused.

I swallow hard and want to laugh at his question. Want to ask if he is joking. He knows I have seen this a hundred plus times. I have most of the lines memorized. Have backup DVDs in case one gets scratched. But he knows how much I love it, so I don't laugh. He watches them over and over with me because of how he feels for me. If that isn't some form of love, I don't know what is.

Reaching up, I thread my fingers through his hair and lean forward, bringing my lips to his. My top leg wiggles between his as he throws his over my hip, pulling me closer. We have made out on the couch before—at my house and his—but today feels different. More heated. More intense. A desire to go further. To take the next step.

His hand dips under my shirt and he grazes my navel with the tops of his short nails. The stroke has me drawing back and gasping. A second later, I bring my lips back to his in a frenzy. My hands roam his face, his neck, his chest through the cotton rock band tee. When I reach his waist, my fingertips tickle along the skin there, eliciting a hiss from his lips.

The urge to take it further lingers in the gravity surrounding us. Weighs us down. Both of us greedy. The fire. The hunger. The raw intensity of lust and desire. It drives us forward. As much as I have thought about waiting until we are a little older, I can't deny how much I want him in this moment. And if I want him like this, I can only imagine what he must be feeling.

But he breaks the kiss. Our breaths panting, hearts hammering. And neither one of us can shift our eyes from the other.

"Do you not want to…" I leave the question unfinished, unsure if this is something he wants. He has as much of a choice to make as I do.

He catches the worry on my face and his answer is immediate. "I do. Believe me, I do. It's just… what if your parents come home? That'd be a moment no one would ever forget. Plus" —he sweeps a few straggler hairs aside— "I'd like our first time to be more special than the couch while watching a movie. Not that we have to plan it, but it's a big deal. For both of us."

He makes a valid point. But I can't help the rapid-fire

pulse banging in my chest right now. Or the intense craving that grows low in my belly. "I guess you're right. But can we keep making out? I was enjoying myself immensely."

His laugh is loud and throaty and vibrates against my chest as he brings me closer to him. "Sorry I cut you off, baby."

And then he leans down, brings my mouth back to his and we get lost in each other for the remainder of the movie. Arms and legs, hands and fingers, feet in tangles, skin touching skin. It's hot and needy and all-consuming. When the credits scroll up the screen, we have to tear ourselves away from each other. Gasping and overheated.

Everything is perfect. Everything is wonderful. And I pray it will be like this forever.

TWENTY-THREE

CORA

Present

CAN exhaustion and jubilation go hand in hand? Most days I would answer with a resolute no. Absolutely not.

But today, after only five hours of sleep, I haven't stopped smiling since my eyes opened. It was the first reaction I had when my alarm sounded. Made brushing my teeth a bit more challenging. Even Luna noticed the difference in my demeanor when I poured kibble into her bowl, her furry little body weaving between my legs and purring loudly. If her mama is happy, she is happy.

The young woman behind the counter at the juice bar hands me my coffee and a small brown bag containing my coconut bowl. I sip the delicious brew before exiting and hopping back in my car. Before starting up the engine, I steal a quick bite of my bowl and relish in the creaminess.

The drive from Main Street to Causeway Boulevard is brief, loaded with sights and people. Runners and cyclists and families. Parks and playgrounds and golfers. One of my favorite parts of Dunedin is the small-town vibe. Everyone here is friendly. The town bursts with energy. Events pop up every weekend, if not more frequently. Not every city has the same community atmosphere. It is invigorating and refreshing to know places like this still exist.

The line to get into the state park is long, as is typical on a beautiful day like today. I pay the attendant and drive into the park, heading for the agreed-upon meeting location. Blue skies with sparse clouds make up the view as a gentle breeze blows through my rolled down windows. The trees lining the road inside the park sway and glow under the beaming sunlight. This time of year is when my slice of Florida is perfect. A slight coolness with a ghost of the summer to come.

Parking under a small, rare patch of shade with my car backed in, I scan the lot for Alyson's rental. When I don't see it, I retrieve my bowl and enjoy my breakfast while waiting for her and Gavin to arrive. Rock music vibrates through the speakers around me. Five bites from finishing and three songs later, Alyson and Gavin drive through the lot in search of a space.

Dark sunglasses mask Gavin's eyes from the world,

his head pressed against the headrest. I imagine he is as tired as I am. No doubt his eyes are closed behind the lenses. We have exhausted each other, but are taking things in stride this week. I wouldn't change any of it. More than happy to have exhaustion bleeding through my veins if things between us will shift for the better. Head back down the path we once traveled.

"God, I missed him," I whisper to myself.

Although I haven't dreamed it for two or three years, envisioning Gavin in my arms again has been something I never let go of. How could I let him go completely? How could I wipe away what we had? Our history… we didn't just share the best two years of my teenage life. Two years that tattooed every perfect moment and emotion on my heart. Every important exchange between two people in a relationship, we had every single of those experiences together. First legitimate relationship. First real kiss. And sex… no one ever forgets their first. He was mine and I his. And no one can change any of that. No one can rewrite our firsts.

When he left, I was certain he would come back as soon as he could. We had it all planned out. Down to the very last detail. Or so we thought. But when you're young, and can't pay to travel across the country, plans change. Promises slip through the cracks. People fade into the background.

Alyson parks three spaces down and across from me. I sit in my car a minute longer, watching from the driver's seat as Gavin gets out of the car and scans the parking lot, a hand hovering above his sunglasses. The moment he spots my car, his shaded eyes landing on mine, a monumental smile stretches across his face.

"Damn," I whisper on a sigh.

I have only seen this smile a few times from him, including the one he gifts me now. It echoes off him, bounces through the atmosphere, and hits me with a force that knocks me breathless. My lips part as I suck in a breath, his eyes not missing the effect he has on me—even fifty feet away—causing his smile to brighten further.

Walking with a bounce in his stride, he sidles up to my door and pokes his head through the open window. "Good morning, baby." His lips warm against my neck as he imprints his lips on the skin below my ear.

An audible sigh exhales from my chest as my eyes roll back before my lids shut out the world around us. Heat fires in my chest; surging, rising, spreading to every nerve ending in my body. His lips and tongue travel a path along the curve of my neck. All coherent thoughts vanish and I melt into a puddle in my car.

A cough from behind him interrupts the moment and snaps us both back to the reason why we are here. My eyes flick to Gavin's, his happiness reflecting my beaming smile. "Good morning," I say, breathless.

"Shouldn't we get started?" Alyson gripes, a hint of irritation in her voice.

"Yes. Sorry," I apologize, rolling up my windows and stepping out of the car. "Let me grab my equipment from the back and then we can start."

She nods, then asks, "Where's your assistant? Do we need to wait for her too?" Her tone transitions from irritation to annoyance in point-five seconds.

What crawled up her ass and died?

"Erin won't be here today. Minimal equipment is necessary for today's shoot. Plus, she had a prior engagement." My tone is courteous, when all I want is to give her the same level of shit she dishes out to me. But, as always, I take the higher ground.

She starts walking toward her car, speaking over her shoulder at us. "I'm grabbing my bag from the car. Be ready when I walk back over."

As soon as she is out of earshot, I glance up at Gavin, silently asking why the hell Alyson is being a top-notch bitch to me today. Lifting the hatch on the back, I grab the cameras I plan to use today, hooking the straps over my head.

Seconds pass before he speaks up, his voice raspy and low. "She's upset with me. This morning, I broke the news to her that I plan to move back to Florida. She knows I still want her as my agent, but isn't thrilled with the idea of doing the job from the other side of the country."

Hanging my head, I mumble, "So, this is also about me. Her frustration isn't just with you, but also with me.

Am I right?" I hate that us being together will cause a rift in his career.

He brushes my hair behind my ear and follows the gesture with his eyes. "I didn't mention you when I spoke with her earlier. But I'm sure she put two and two together with my greeting you. None of that matters, though. I'll talk with her. Explain things she knows nothing about."

My chest tightens as guilt riddles me. I don't want animosity—between him and his agent or me, by proxy. "Okay. But, Gavin…" I pause and he locks his gaze on mine. "Please don't make me the sole reason you return."

He cocks his head and studies me a minute. His eyes narrow then relax behind his sunglasses as he starts to shake his head. "You don't get it, do you?"

"Get what?" I furrow my brows, obviously unaware. A small piece of my heart tells me I know the answer. Whispers it softly in my ear. But the gut-wrenching memories step out of the shadows and remind me to never assume. Assumptions kill dreams and crush hearts.

"It has always been about you. It always will be."

"Gavin…" He can't say things like that. Not unless he is prepared to back every sentiment. And not with more words or promises, but with actions. Actions are what I need.

His fingers brush along my jawline, from my temple

to my chin. "You don't get it, baby. I have missed you every day since the moment my mom packed our life up and moved us away. It's been four thousand six hundred and ninety-eight days, Cora. And until I'm back here, with you beside me again, I won't stop counting. Because it's the only thing that gives me hope."

My throat squeezes at his words, making it hard to swallow the lump building from emotional overload. Making it difficult to breathe. How do I follow up after he confesses facts so heavy? Anything I say after seems minuscule. But not responding makes me an asshole. Just as I am about to formulate a response, about to use my words, Alyson steps up to us and huffs.

"You two ready? The day won't last forever," Alyson snaps.

"Yep," I snap in return. "Just discussing things while we waited for you." I am over her shit already. It is too damn early to be bitter, but my lack of sleep is making me grouchier than usual. "Follow me," I command, turning and walking away, not looking to see if either of them follows.

I understand her pissy state—I do. But being a bitch because someone chooses their happiness over yours is just plain shitty. Yeah, her job won't be as easy going forward, but it's manageable. Several professions nowadays don't require people to reside in the same city, let alone state.

We walk a while, maybe thirty minutes. None of us

mutters a word. The silence between the three of us borders on awkward. But the quiet gives me time to replay Gavin's earlier confession. To come to the realization that he has missed me more than I previously suspected. But if he has pined for me all these years, why has he not done anything to remedy it? Why didn't he reach out to me? He should have at least tried to explain what changed. It makes no sense. In the beginning, sure. Neither of us had the means to visit each other. But if he has wanted to return so badly, what has stopped him? His job? His mom? Maybe someone else?

The thought of another woman being the reason has my stomach churning. No doubt Gavin spent time with or dated other women over the last thirteen years. I'd be shocked if he hadn't. But the idea of him being in a relationship *now* has bile coating my throat. So, I shove it aside and file it in the *ask Gavin later* part of my mind.

A quarter mile down the trail, I stop in my tracks, and Gavin runs into my backside.

"Sorry," I mutter. "I should've said something to let you know we were here."

"It's okay, baby." He kisses my temple before correcting his stance.

Behind us, I hear Alyson huff and mumble something under her breath. Honestly, if she doesn't chill the hell out, I am going to open my mouth and bark out things I cannot take back. I won't regret a single word, but they will reflect poorly on my professionalism. And today is not the day to test my sanity.

Alyson slides a collapsible chair from a bag, opens it and plops down. After a minute, her focus shifts from me and Gavin to her incessantly dinging cell phone. Whatever keeps her attention focused elsewhere is good with me. Because every ounce of my rational side prays she remains silent the entire shoot. For her sake and mine.

This section of the trail is near the water, so we have the ability to get photos in the greenery, near the water, and a combination of both. The location is absolutely perfect. Not only for the scenery, but also because today's shoot entails more skin. More skin than I typically shoot. More skin than I have probably seen on another guy in years. And not just any skin, but Gavin's skin.

Please, powers that be, let me make it through today without doing or saying something stupid. Please.

Hence the need for partial seclusion. Alyson is nearby, but not close enough to see us in clear view. Let alone, hear us.

Don't get me wrong, I have taken intimate pictures before. Couples who wanted to capture special moments such as pregnancy. Women—and men—who wanted to do something special for their significant other such as boudoir sessions. Boudoir sessions are the extent of the raciness in my portfolio. And they were saucy, steamy, and intimate as hell, but very different from this.

Because this is Gavin. The only guy I have loved. The only person I have imagined having a future with. And the one guy who ran away with my heart thirteen years ago and held it hostage.

The first shots are simplistic. Him in board shorts against the foliage backdrop. Some with the waterfront at his backside. All reflecting the strength of his chest and arms without flaunting it. The shorts rest low on his hips, the definition of his lower abdominals peeking at the front of the waistband. I swallow and do my best to maintain composure. After I'm satisfied with the number of shots taken with all backdrops, we prep for the next set of photos.

When he drops his shorts, and I glimpse the thick-banded boxer briefs hugging his toned gluts and upper quads, I swallow. Hard. My insides swirl with a new thread of desire. My thighs clench together as I gawk at the outline of him in the branded underwear. And for a moment, I forget I am here to do a job.

I am so fucked.

When my eyes come back to his, a teasing smile occupies his face. Not only was I checking out the lines and definitions of his body, but I was caught doing so. And he is eating it up.

Should I be embarrassed? Normally, the answer would be one-hundred-percent yes. If it were any other client, I would be apologizing endlessly. But with Gavin, I wear my ogling with pride. It's difficult not to smile back at him. And let's get real, Gavin is hot as hell.

Bringing the camera to my eye, I flush as I stare through the lens. He is enjoying this way too much. It is written all over him—how he flexes his muscles and contorts his body, how he eats me alive with his eyes, and how the prideful smirk refuses to leave his lips. I inhale deep, realizing I have had the camera pressed to my face for more than a minute without taking a single photo.

And he knows it.

"See something you like, baby?" His smugness penetrates the air and drifts my way.

Don't answer him. Stay strong. Keep your mouth shut. Don't...

"Maybe," I tease. "Still up for debate."

His laugh pierces the silence of the pathway and echoes through the trees and out to the water. While not posing, I hold down the shutter and capture Gavin in his natural state. Candid photos have always been my favorite, although most of them are kept in my own private collection. The shots just taken will more than likely never leave my laptop. And I will enjoy them for years to come.

After we capture enough shots along the path, we walk to the small section of beach. Some poses on the sand before he enters the water. Several poses while he is in the water, the waistband and a couple inches of the cotton below it visible. And then he strolls out of the water, prepared for the shots of him lying wet in the sand near the surf.

In this moment, three things hit me with complete clarity.

1. Gavin is wearing white underwear.
2. The fabric isn't as thick as I originally thought.
3. Gavin is hard as steel as he walks toward me with a shit-eating grin on his face.

I can't breathe. Can't speak. Am rendered immobile. My face is hot, and not from the sun beaming down on us for hours. My limbs have forgotten how to function and my jaw is stuck in the open position.

Breathe, Cora. Inhale… Exhale… You can do this.

I can't do this.

Shit. Fuck. Damn.

The camera hangs suspended in my hand, just below my rosy face, as my sole focus is on his body. Yes, my eyes are zeroed in on the girth below the now see-through cotton. But my periphery catches the ripples of his lower abdomen, his V more visible and pointing directly at his pot of gold at the end of the rainbow.

It's not as if this is the first time I have seen Gavin in all his glory. But the last time I saw him anywhere remotely close to naked, we were sixteen and his body looked nothing like the one before me. The Gavin from my memories is good-looking and desirable and made my heart sing.

But this older version of Gavin...

Heat rises in my chest, trickling throughout my torso and seeping into my limbs. It isn't as simple as me being turned on by his appearance—I have seen numerous attractive men over the years that never sparked this incendiary feeling inside me. Part of it is visual, but another part is the knowledge that he only has eyes for me. That he only wants me. That every part of him is reserved for me.

"You okay, baby? You look a little heated," he teases then adds a soft chuckle. "We can take a break. Grab some water."

I stick my tongue out at him as if we are kids again, following it up with a goofy face. Bringing the camera to my eye, I drag in a deep breath.

This is work, Cora. Focus on the work aspect.

"Nope. I'm good," I tell him, coughing to clear my throat. "Although, I'm not sure how many of these shots will be usable."

Through the lens, I see his head cock to the side as his brows pinch together. The shutter closes at a rapid-fire pace, photo after photo taken and stored on the SD card. He steps closer and closer as I try to focus the lens higher and higher.

A hundred or so frames later, Gavin speaks up. "Why?"

For a moment, I am confused by his question. Not sure what he is asking about. "Why what?"

"Why won't some of the shots be usable?"

I continue shooting as I speak, not taking my eye away from the viewfinder. "Well, from what I've been told, this shoot is for magazines everywhere. An ad campaign for the clothing and accessories."

He nods. "Yeah. So?"

"And I think it's meant to reach a wide age range, starting with teens."

"Okay…"

He is not picking up on this. Not one bit. And damnit, I am going to have to come right out and say it. Internally, my hand slaps my forehead. *Just say it. We are both adults, for fuck's sake.*

"Gavin, parents won't want their teenage kids looking at an ad where the model has an erection, which is one-hundred-percent visible through the wet material. Many of the older female population may enjoy it, maybe some men too, but that won't be the only eyes on the ad."

His laugh is throaty, his abs contracting in ways that coil my insides tight. I continue taking photo after photo, capturing more candid shots. When he finishes laughing, he walks the small distance to me. My camera still glued to my face as he approaches, snapping as many photos as possible. He slowly pushes the camera aside and tips my chin up so we are eye to eye.

"Do you know how *hard* it is to stand practically naked in front of you? Knowing your job is to look at me. To take photos of me. Your visual assessment has me hungrier for you with each press of the shutter release."

I swallow hard, the sound from the action echoes loud in my head and I wonder if he hears it too. His pupils dilate more, his steely-gray irises darkening with each passing second. If he believes it is challenging to be in front of the camera, he has no idea how difficult it is to be on the other side. To view him through the lens and attempt to keep every thought I have as practiced as possible. To remind myself I am working and to be on my best behavior.

"It's not so easy from where I'm standing either. Having to maintain complete photographer-client idiosyncrasies while I snap photos of the one person who incinerates my insides. When—right now—the only thing I want to do is trace my fingers over every line of your body."

Neither of us looks away. His chest rises and falls faster with each breath he takes. The friction of his chest brushing against my nipples builds a delicious, insatiable heat between my legs. Right here, on the white sands of the small beachfront, I want him to kiss me. Want to feel the heat of his lips brush against mine. Against my skin, down my throat and…

A cough rings out behind me, and I snap out of my fantasy. Gavin peeks over my head, his smile faltering when he sees who stands there. Only one possible person could be there. Alyson. And from the scene she walked in on, I would not be shocked if she policed the rest of the shoot.

Gavin's eyes come back to mine before he bends to press a soft kiss on my lips. "I'll try to think about something else so we can wrap this up."

I nod, blurting, "shitty diapers."

He tips his head in question. "Shitty diapers…" he says, dragging out the words.

"Yeah. Think about that and it'll solve the current *setback.*"

He walks backward, a hearty laugh bellowing from his chest. "You always know the right thing to say."

We hike back to the cars, Alyson leading the way twenty feet ahead of us and griping over how blood-thirsty the insects are in Florida. Gavin falls in step beside me, his fingers wrapped around mine and clutching me as if I might slip away. Not a single word is spoken for ten minutes as we follow the trail.

When we reach the opening, I hear Alyson mutter *thank God* under her breath. Gavin laughs loud enough for only me to hear, shaking his head at her bitching. Obviously, the mosquito population isn't as predominant in California. Seeing as summer exists the majority of the year in Florida, I would not be shocked if mosquitos were dubbed the state insect one day.

Once we are back in the lot, Alyson walks over to her rental, but not before sending a knowing look to Gavin. A look that says she understands, but also not to push her boundaries. What those boundaries are, I am not privy to.

I press the unlock button on my key fob, lifting the hatch and tucking my cameras into the bags under the cover. Gavin stands inches away as his gaze sears me. After everything is in its rightful place, I step back and close the hatch. When I turn to face Gavin, my eyes roam his body. Starting at the waistband of his board shorts—which barely hang on his hips—trailing up the grooves and curves of his abdomen, falling on his pecs—where my mouth waters at the sight of the barbells through his nipples—rising up his throat. I watch his Adam's apple bob as my eyes scrape over his stubble and lips, and eventually land on eyes that want to devour me.

Fuck me.

His expression says everything his mouth is not. The way his tongue jets out and swipes along his bottom lip before he clamps it between his teeth. The slight smirk that follows. How his irises shift from steel to pewter. A slight rise and fall of his shoulders as his breath comes faster. How his pulse noticeably pumps harder in that spot just below his ear.

Not only does he want to kiss me. He wants to peel away my shorts and tank. But he also aches to run his fingers through my hair, ball them into fists and yank the strands taught against my scalp. To see my body bow and plead for his touch, his mouth, his tongue. Along every inch of my skin, rebranding and rememorizing all the places he has been once before.

Both of us stand stock-still. Not touching. Not speaking. Sharing a bond our bodies and hearts have never forgotten. The void between us grows less dark and vacant with each passing second.

He flings the shirt he's been holding over his shoulder, sliding his sunglasses down and shielding his eyes from the sun. "Have dinner with me tonight," he states. It is not a question, but also not a command.

Every coherent thought in my mind screams at me to tell him no. That we shouldn't be doing things together as if we are a couple. At least not until this shoot is over and I know I'm not throwing my heart on the line. My brain fights with my heart—battles with my soul—and tells me to be rational, to think this through and understand the repercussions if something goes amiss.

But I ignore my brain. Tell it to shut the hell up and let me live in the moment. Because it has been so long since I have lived in the moment. Or lived life to its fullest. And I am tired of hiding—who I am and what I want. Tired of missing out on life and love.

"Yes." It's all I say. Because I don't trust myself to say anything else right now. If I open my mouth, I may say words I said once before but should wait to say again.

His body comes alive and his expression mirrors a jubilance I have not seen in ages. It rolls off him in waves, piercing my aura and infecting me with a dose. I cannot help but smile at his behavior, his energy, his life force.

"Any requests? I'm open to whatever," he says.

Feigning indecision, I tap a finger against my lips. If Gavin remembers anything about me at all, he would know my answer. But for good measure, I drag out my supposed thinking. When I feel I have sufficiently tortured him enough, I answer.

"Maybe we could grab some Asian," I suggest, biting my lower lip.

A laugh rips from his throat as he shakes from head to toe. "I should have known that would be your answer," he chuckles out. "Anywhere in particular you'd like to go?"

"How about I figure that part out, seeing as I'm more familiar with the area. Want me to pick you up?"

"It wouldn't be a proper date if you're the one picking me up. How about I meet you at your place and we drive from there?"

"Seriously? We're almost thirty and it's the twenty-first century. Women can pick up men for a date."

He nods, his laugh sparking back to life. "I realize what era we live in, baby. Doesn't mean I can't try to be somewhat of a gentleman. Even if I don't have my car with me. But I'll find a way to get there, then you can take the helm."

I walk to the driver's side door, Gavin a step behind me with his hand on my hip. Opening the door, I toss my phone on the seat before turning to face him and say goodbye. When I turn, his face is a breath from mine. His lips hovering dangerously close and his eyes locked with determination. As he leans closer, my eyes close, my body ready and waiting to feel his lips on mine. Just as warmth paints my lips, Alyson honks the rental's horn.

"Let's go!" she hollers.

And just like that, she has plucked my last nerve today. I swallow it down and don't let it ruin the moment.

Reluctantly, we pull apart. Our bodies now separated by feet rather than inches. But the vibrating energy between us remains. Almost like when we were teens and our parents walked in the room.

His hand squeezes my hip. "I'll see you later, baby. Is five thirty okay?"

"That's fine. See you then," I say as he releases my hip and walks away.

Immobile, I watch as he gets into the car and Alyson

backs out. He gives me a sweet half smile as they drive past me. The car leaves the lot, drives on the paved two-lane road and heads for the exit. It's not until the car is out of sight that I slide into my car, start the engine and roll down the windows. And as I drive out of the park, my mind drifts over all the possibilities of what tonight means. For us. For our future.

This is really happening. The only person I have ever truly loved is back in my life. And he has promised to return to me. To stay with me. To keep me forever.

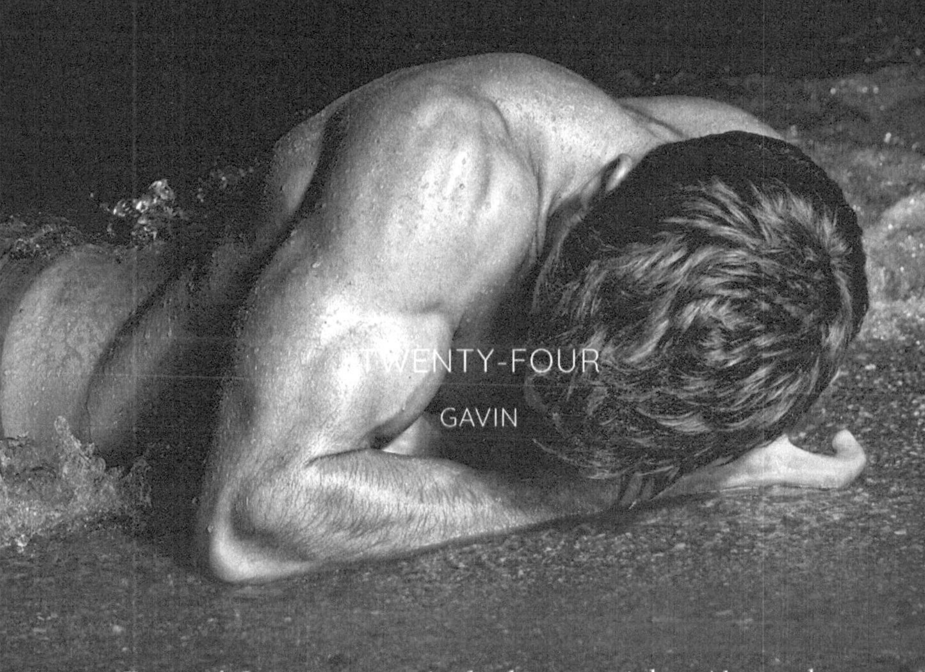

TWENTY-FOUR

GAVIN

Fuck if I am not excited about tonight. About the possibility of a future with the one person who has been tattooed on my heart for more than a decade. The one person I never want to be apart from again. The one person I cannot wait to spend every day of forever with.

The entire way back to the hotel, Alyson chews me a new asshole. Bitching and moaning about how I need to be more mindful in regards to my actions. Scolding me worse than any occasion my parents did. And how I better not forget I am under contract—with her, the clothing designer and the magazine. As if I need reminding. As if this is my first shoot.

I let her have her moment. Allow her to complain and reiterate the same shit on repeat. Spew the same garbage she has since the first day of the shoot. But when she finishes, I take it as a sign that I finally get a chance to speak. To tell her what is on my mind. To shut down her tirade.

"Alyson, you know how much I value your opinion and expertise. But there are a few parts of my life that are *not* what *I* pay *you* to handle. My love life is not part of your job and most definitely will never be a part of your pay grade. Do you understand?"

There is no plainer way to express this to her. I only hope she gets where I am coming from. That I am not trying to be a dick and just laying the basics out there. She needs to understand me being with Cora is permanent. She needs to get used to us being together and me living my life how I want.

We drive south on Edgewater, not far from the Dunedin-Clearwater border. "Of course, I understand. But you pay me to make decisions that will impact the future of your career. And this" —she gestures behind us — "her, will impact your future. In more ways than one."

That is what I am hoping.

"I realize she'll change my future. It's what I'm hoping for. The one thing I've wanted for years. And now I have the ability of returning to her." I pause a moment and ponder over my next words. "This will make things different with our relationship, but you can either represent me from afar or I can find someone else. The choice is yours."

I hate to throw ultimatums on the table, but I will not have her or anyone else hindering my return. Not

Alyson. Not my mother. No one. Although, a small part of me thinks my mom may be happy for me. After our move to Cali, I witnessed how sad she was for me. How guilty she felt for removing me from my friends and girlfriend. It hurt me, and her by proxy.

"Well, aside from your plan to move—" she says hesitantly, then continues. "—don't forget about the shoot you have booked with Layla. And speaking of Layla, how will all of that work out if you move across the country?"

I shoot her a pointed look, but she doesn't catch it with her eyes on the road. "I'll talk with her. She'll understand. Besides, she's good now."

"I hope you're right."

"What's that supposed to mean?" I question, fire building in my chest. I am so over Alyson, her selfishness and her annoyance with me living my life how I choose.

"Nothing. All it means is I hope it doesn't ruin you or her."

"It won't," I snap. Alyson is grasping at straws. Trying to make something of nothing. Trying to rile me up. But I won't feed into her line of bullshit.

The remainder of our drive is quiet. Alyson churning my words in her head, realizing she has an important decision to make. She is either on board or she isn't. And trying to throw bullshit about Layla in the mix—it is a low blow, even for Alyson. I have been working for years to get to this point. To return to Cora. And now that I am able, nothing will stop me. Nothing will take this away from me. From us.

The Uber driver dropped me off in front of Cora's house five minutes ago. So why am I standing out front? My feet locked in place on the rustic paver pathway leading to her front stoop. I stare at the gray siding, black shutters, and black-framed glass door, taking my first, true assessment of her home.

A large oak tree shadows most of the yard with lush ferns growing around the base of the trunk. Two ducks waddle away from the ferns and cross the street to head for the park's pond. A brick chimney painted dark gray crawls up the eastern wall of the house—and although fireplaces aren't used often in Florida, I bet she uses it every chance she gets. Small flowered plants encompass the border of the house—pops of yellow and red and purple in the foliage—white rocks at their base. Large windows take up the majority of the exterior walls and allow for hours of natural light. Strands of starry lights dangle from the roof over the stoop. Everything about this house screams her style. Simple.

Clean-cut. Monochromatic. With the exception of the colorful plants.

I remain rooted another minute before dragging in a deep breath. The reality of us coming back together hits me like a lead weight. A burning tightness takes residence in my chest, building and expanding with every breath. It consumes every molecule of oxygen, every drop of blood, every fiber and jolts me back to life.

This is my future. She is my future.

God, I have dreamed about this moment for so long. Dreamed of her in my arms again. Imagined what life would be like waking up in the same bed every day. Moving around each other in the kitchen while making breakfast. Spooning on the couch as we watch movies in the dark. Discussing our day over dinner. Laughing together with friends. Creating a family and growing old together.

She is it for me. Always has been. Always will be. Not a single day has passed where I haven't thought of Cora. Wondered what she was doing. How she fit into the world now. If she still thought of me. If she would be able to love me again.

Fuck, I love her so much.

The front door opens and Cora stands in the doorway looking at me with questions in her eyes. "You okay?" she asks, doubt in her voice. No doubt she has seen me standing out here. Hopefully not for too long.

"Yeah. Sorry." I stride up the path and stop in front of

her. I plant a kiss on her forehead and inhale deeply, filling my nose with the scent that is one-hundred-percent her. "Was just admiring your house. You've done so well for yourself. And it suits you so much."

"Thank you," she says, a timid smile pushing up her cheeks. "You coming in? Or do you plan to stand out here until we leave?"

I step past her, seeing the inside of her house in a new light. The interior isn't overly spacious, but it is enough for her. *For us.* I love how easily I picture our future. Our road may have had major detours, but we are finally coming back to the path we belong on. *Together.*

To the right, the living room—maybe twelve square-feet—showcases the fireplace from the eastern wall with a charcoal and gray fabric couch opposite. A resin-coated wood slice coffee table rests between the two, decorated with a wide bowl of succulents. To the left is the kitchen and dining area. The kitchen is small yet vast. A large fridge at one end, the range near the other end. On the small island sitting between the kitchen and dining is a farmhouse sink and enough space for a few people to sit on stools and eat at the bar. Planked wood and riveted steel make up the dining table with four seats attached that swing underneath. Along the far wall of the dining area is her desk—a restored piece with distressed black paint and two shallow drawers. Simplistic art decorates the walls while minimal pieces adorn the furniture. With a tall vaulted ceiling, the cozy house is more spacious than it would appear from the outside.

I smile as I take it all in. There is not one part of this house that doesn't have a piece of her in its grain or plaster or beams. Without a doubt, I would recognize this place as hers in a heartbeat. Her style screams from every nook and cranny. Her predilection for minimalism and simplicity shine from every corner, wall, and piece of décor.

"I was almost finished getting ready when I saw you outside. Give me a minute and then we can go."

"Take all the time you need, baby. I'll be out here waiting," I say as I sit on the couch.

Seconds after I sit, an all-black cat jumps up beside me, purring and rubbing its head on my arm. I scratch and pet the cat as it takes a liking to me. *Glad you like me because I will be around quite often.*

"And that would be Luna," Cora shares. "She's a lover and will probably coat you in her fur before we leave. Good thing I own several lint rollers."

I laugh as I pet Luna and she loves on me further. As I stroke her soft fur, the thought of her one day being *my* Luna brings a smile to my face. Since becoming a model, I have never owned a pet. As much as I wanted one, the thought of leaving a dog or cat behind for weeks on end doesn't sit well with me. It would be unfair to them, and me, to have someone pet sit and me not spend time with them. They may not be human, but they are your children all the same.

Cora breaks my introspection when she walks back into the room. "Ready when you are. Unless you'd rather spend date night with Luna," she says and giggles, a sound I haven't heard in so long. I almost forgot how musical her laugh is. Almost.

Patting Luna's backside, I whisper my apologies to her before rising from the couch. "Lead the way, baby."

We head out the back door, get in her car and drive to dinner. A little over thirty minutes later, we pull into a small parking lot beside an Asian vegan restaurant. She leads us inside and I love it immediately. The restaurant is small and simple, low-key. Absolutely perfect.

Once we are seated, we look over the menu and choose a few appetizers as well as our meals. We talk about life and key things that have happened to us over the last thirteen years. And as awkward as it is, we discuss relationships we have had. Funny enough, neither of us has had a relationship that lasted more than a few months. Neither of us finding someone who fulfilled us in the same way we do each other. And to me, that speaks volumes.

I share with her my plan to move back after the shoot in Cali and how I will still be able to work being out here. She points out why she is skeptical it will work—not us, but me working. That I won't have the same connections as I do now. But I beg to differ. Since I have been working in the industry for the last ten years, I have developed several contacts and am able to find work whenever and wherever I choose. And moving to Florida, I will end up discovering a whole new array of connections. Ones I would never have in California. Tampa, Orlando, and Miami are major cities picking up steam in the modeling industry.

The rest of dinner goes by seamlessly. Conversations about both of our work lives cease. We pack up our leftovers and I pay the bill. Soon thereafter, we are on our way back to her house. The drive back absent of conversation as we listen to music and enjoy the feel of our fingers laced together. And when we park in her driveway, the atmosphere between us grows heavy. With questions. With uncertainty. And most of all… desire.

Thirteen and a half years ago

As DORKY AS IT SOUNDS, I can't wait to celebrate our one-year anniversary together. Although we have been best friends for the last year and a half, we weren't dubbed "official" until this time last year. Most people assume it is only the girl who gets excited about these moments. But I am buzzing with the thrill and ready to celebrate with the one person who means the world to me.

Brakes squeak as Cora parks in the driveway, the new-to-her Toyota a little rumbly. Her parents bought her the used car a couple weeks ago after she officially got her license. It has been great to be able to do our own thing, within reason, and not be subjected to our parents taking us places or annoying older friends with cars.

I run out the front door, yelling to my parents that I will be home by curfew. Swinging open the passenger door with a bit more oomph than expected, I slip into the seat, lean over the center console and kiss my girl breathless. When we come up for air, I stare at the hazy expression on her face. It is a dash of euphoria mixed with the soft lines of her angelic face. And I never tire of seeing her this way. Happy.

"You can't do that," she whispers, her eyes hidden behind her lids.

Leaning back into her space, my lips hover a breath from hers. "Can't do what, baby?"

"Kiss me like that and expect me to be able to function afterward."

I press a soft, chaste kiss to her lips. "How can I not kiss you like you hold the other half of my soul?"

Her eyes flick open, her green irises shimmering in the fading light of the day. Darting back and forth between mine, her eyes expressive in their desire to know how we could both feel the way we do. We idle in the driveway another minute, the car vibrating beneath us, as so many things are said without a single word spoken. How is it I know everything she is thinking without her even telling me?

The answer is simple really. Cora is my home. She is the one place where I feel most at ease. The one person I can be myself around and never feel a sense of shame or reservation or judgment. She makes my breathing spike and my heart soar. And her fingers on me… her touch is lightning in my veins.

There is no other person I could imagine spending my life with. I may be only fifteen—almost sixteen—and less experienced with life, but this fact is etched in my bones. Carved since the day I was born. Not just for me, but for her as well.

After a moment, she drags in a breath and faces the steering wheel. "You ready?" she asks, her voice unsteady.

"As ready as I'll ever be."

Rock music spills out of the speakers as we drive toward Indian Rocks Beach. For our one-year anniversary, we decided to go to a small Italian restaurant between the beach and intercoastal. Asian food is Cora's version of crack, but she wanted to do something different tonight. And as many times as I told her we could go to our favorite Thai or Japanese restaurant, she gracefully suggested we go somewhere new.

To create a new memory for this milestone moment. A memory we will never forget. I wanted to tell her there is no way I would ever forget any minute involving her.

Pulling into the parking lot, she finds a space and parks. We get out of the car and it is the first time tonight I get the opportunity to see what she wears. Part of me is shocked, while another part of me is turned on.

For the first time ever, Cora is in a dress. Her usual denim bottoms and cotton graphic tee are nowhere to be found. But this dress suits her. In more ways than one. The fabric clings to her like a second skin, accentuating all the curves lying beneath. Curves I have touched, but not really seen altogether. Nestled in the black material are small shapes I can't make out from where I stand. As I inch closer to her, looping her arm in mine, I see the shapes are cat faces. From afar, anyone could misconstrue them as polka dots. Her dress is the perfect mix of black, rock and Cora.

"You look beautiful," I tell her, planting a kiss at her temple.

"Thank you. You're looking pretty good yourself."

To be honest, I feel underdressed next to her. In a pair of black jeans and a navy button-down with the cuffs rolled to my elbows, this is the most dressed up I have been since I was little and my mom dressed me for special occasions. It isn't that I don't look nice, but Cora is stunning.

The hostess walks us to our table, a flickering votive candle and a small vase holding two red roses rest in the center. Our server greets and informs us of the specials for the evening, then takes our drink orders and disappears. We are both silent as we look over the menu, my mouth watering at all the delicious options. In my periphery, I catch Cora setting her menu down.

"Do you know what you're having?" I inquire.

"Yeah. I was tossed up between the spaghetti carbonara and the gnocchi a la Villa Gallace. They both sound amazing, but I think I'll get the carbonara. You want to share the Caesar salad for two?"

"Caesar sounds good. I'm still on the fence. Lasagna or rigatoni Bolognese?" I look to her for guidance.

"Ooh, that's a tough call," she says, tapping a finger against her pushed out lips. "Layers or tubes, layers or tubes." She bobs her head side to side as she tries to help me decide. "Tubes," she exclaims. "That's what I would choose."

"Tubes for the win!" I belt out a little too loud, mouthing my apologies to the other patrons when they look at me. "Oops," I whisper, both of us laughing with hands over our mouths.

Our server returns, setting our drinks and a basket of bread with garlic and herb oil on the table, then takes our order. When he walks away, we simply gaze at one another. In the time since Cora and I first met, we have learned we don't need to fill time by talking about things that don't hold value to us. We have a bond, a language all our own. Words don't need to be spoken. *We just know.* I stretch my hand across the table and she places hers in mine. Connected. Everything is always better when we are connected.

Our dinner arrives and we dive right in. On the small bread plates, we each portion our dish and pass it to the other. As we eat, we talk about school and friends and our plans during the summer. When we finish, I pay the bill and we leave the restaurant.

Cora drives the car to a beach access parking lot on the other side of the two-lane street. This time of day is generally busy and it can be challenging to find a space, but we land one and make our way to the sand. Just before we step onto the beach, both of us slip our shoes off and carry them as we stroll onto the warmed, soft grains.

After walking for five minutes, we locate a spot where no one obstructs the view in front of us. Plopping down on the sand, Cora leans into me as we watch the sunset. We had timed dinner perfectly so we wouldn't miss this moment. If you have never watched the sunset along the water's horizon, you have been deprived.

The sunset was a favorite of mine. Sharing it with my girl made it more special.

Right now, the sun radiates a hot orange glow like the sphere of fire it is. The sky surrounding it shifts from a soft blue to a light yellow. And the lower the sun drops on the horizon, the more brilliant the colors. Yellow morphs into faint and then bold oranges. A mixture of orange and pink spark next, filtering between the clouds. Shadows and hints of purple edge the stratocumulus clouds floating above as the sun slowly descends.

When the sun dips below the horizon, the sky still dances with colors and clouds. The visual is magical and I am so lucky I get to share it with someone I love.

I shift and turn to face Cora more, her head lifting from my shoulder. One arm still wrapped around her waist, I bring the other to her face and cup her jaw, brushing my thumb over her lips. "I love you," I whisper.

Just now, it is the first time those words have been said in our relationship, but I mean them with every fiber in my soul. Whether or not she reciprocates doesn't matter. Something inside me yearned to release the sentiment. Like a ticking timebomb would detonate inside me if I held it in any longer.

Her eyes hold mine—unmoving, welling. She kisses my thumb that continues to stroke her lips. "I love you, too." The second those words leave her lips, every single molecule inside me radiates warmth. My soul is complete, whole.

Under the brilliance of the setting sun, I lean in and kiss the hell out of the only person in this world that matters to me. The only girl I will ever say those three miraculous words to. My Cora. My love.

We stumble into Cora's house, giddy as school girls. After our proclamations, we left the beach and headed back to her house to watch a movie since I have a few hours until curfew. No doubt it would be *Lord of the*

Rings again. But I don't care, as long as she is beside me. In my arms.

When I notice all the lights are off, I prompt, "Where are your parents?"

"At some charity function in Tampa. They probably won't be home till close to midnight, if it's anything like last year."

A sudden rush of anxiety trickles up my spine, spreads through my limbs, and explodes beneath my sternum. Today is our anniversary. We are alone. After professing our love for each other. And she is looking at me like she has no desire to watch a movie, but perhaps do something else. Something more.

She stalks closer, locks eyes with me and stops when her chest brushes mine. Her fingers reach out and draw lines down my bicep, my forearm, interlocking our fingers. Heat expands and contracts like a breathing organism in my chest. My breath comes in quick, short bursts as she inches closer and closer. And when she pushes up on her toes and kisses me, I forget how to breathe altogether.

The kiss starts off tender and gentle. She slides her hands back up my arms and laces them behind my neck, toying with the edges of my hair. Her tongue darts out and swipes a slow and sinful line over my lower lip, and I moan at the sensation as I part my lips and invite her in. My arms snake around her waist and draw her impossibly closer. Within seconds, the kiss elevates into more. More heated. More passionate. And I can't get enough of her. Her lips, her warmth, her taste.

We start moving, but I don't open my eyes as she slowly guides us. It seems as if we have been walking for hours when her body weight shifts and we settle in place. Our lips break for a moment, which is exactly when I realize we are in her bedroom. Next to her bed. Dim moonlight illuminates the space between the slats of her blinds. And the sudden proximity to her—in the darkness, in her bedroom—amplifies everything I feel for her.

Standing tall, I gaze down at her as she lies back on the bed, elbows propping her up. I want this—want her—but I need to know she feels the same. That she doesn't feel a sense of obligation to take us to the next level. That she wants to do this of her own volition. I would never pressure her into doing something she isn't ready for. Never.

"Cora…" I rasp, my voice thick with emotion as I draw out her name.

She reaches out her hand, her eyes telling me to take it. Wrapping her fingers with mine, she drags me closer. My knees bump the edge of the bed and sweat breaks out across my skin. "Yes, Gavin."

Yes? As in she is responding to me. Or yes, she wants to do this? Wants to take the next step. Sex. What exactly is she saying yes to?

"Are you sure?" I ask, reluctance in my tone. I don't

want her saying yes because she thinks it's what I want her to say. "Because we don't have to if you're not ready."

Her brilliant green eyes pierce mine, her voice steady and firm when she speaks. "I am sure. I don't think I've ever felt more ready in my life." She gives my hand a gentle tug, signaling me to join her on the bed.

This exact moment has infiltrated my dreams for months. I never knew when it would happen, but the fantasy of it was a regular occurrence. Now that it is happening, I am not sure what to do. My feet remain rooted to the floor as I look down at her on the bed. She wants me as much as I want her, although it may be a bit lopsided in my favor. Am I ready for this? To share this once-in-a-lifetime moment with her? Yes, I have never been more ready. So, why am I not moving? Why can I not put my knee on the bed and crawl my way up her body?

"Gavin?" She peers up at me, confusion furrowing her brow. "Are you okay?"

"Yeah, I'm okay. Just give me a second."

"If you're not—"

I cut her off. "I am. It's just… you don't know how long I've waited for this moment. And now that it's here…" I trail off, not knowing how to explain how overwhelmed and buoyant and in love with her I feel right now.

She rises on the bed, perching up on her knees on the

mattress edge. "We can go slow. Maybe just fool around with clothes on. Go from there."

I nod, inhale deeply and focus on her eyes. The way they glimmer in the dim light in her room. Her lips. And how soft they feel when I press mine against them. The warmth of her hands as she frames my face and leans forward, her breath teasing my lips. Her frankincense and gardenia scent wafts around me and entices me further. Makes my pulse throb in my ears and my heart pound in my chest. Has my breaths coming faster, dizzyingly. And when I lean in to kiss her, we melt together.

Our kiss starts off slow, two sets of soft lips brushing together. Her hands slide down my neck and onto my chest as her delicate fingers separate buttons from fabric. I break out in goose bumps when she spreads the cotton, pushes it down my arms, leaves it to dangle from my waist and exposes my skin. A new form of hunger surges beneath my ribcage and in my groin. The kiss morphs, growing in intensity and becoming more animalistic when her nails scratch light lines down the backside of my torso. I tip my head back and gasp.

She takes hold of my hips and starts to crawl backward on her knees, pulling me on the bed. And this time, I don't stop her. Every part of me is desperate for her. Lips, mouth, tongue, hands… more.

Our kiss never falters as she lies back on the mattress and brings me with her. A frenzy erupts between us, and the urge to taste more of her grows stronger with each passing second.

Breaking the kiss, I paint my lips along her jaw, her ear, down the curve of her neck. Her breath ragged beneath me as her chest rises and falls faster with each taste as I consume every inch of her. Running my hands down the sides of her dress, I slide down her body and begin kissing her ankles, her calves, her thighs. When I reach her dress, I slip my fingers under the hem—warranting a gasp from her—and scoot the material up her body. Cora sits up, helping me lift the tight, stretchy fabric and yanking it off her body.

As her body lands on the mattress again, my dick jolts at the sight of her. Matching black lace covers her breasts and the junction of her thighs, the material sheer enough to see her pert nipples and a thin patch of curls. *Holy shit.*

She wrenches me down, and we are all mouths and tongues and roaming hands. Minutes later, she tosses my shirt away as she unbuttons my jeans and shoves them down my legs. The second my pants hit the floor, my lips move down her chest and explore. My tongue lavishes her nipples before licking its way down her navel and hovering above her panties.

My eyes lock with hers, asking permission. She nods, running her fingers through my hair and tugging. Slipping my thumbs under the elastic, I slide the lacy triangle down her thighs and to the floor. When I come back to her body, I taste her for the first time. Her addictive flavor a blend of salty and sweetness on my tongue. A moan rips from her throat as I melt into her, my dick throbbing between my legs.

"Oh, god…" she garbles.

She is sweeter than any confection I have ever tasted or imagined. But when I kiss my way up her body, and our tongues collide again, I become even hungrier for her. Her hips grind against me, begging for me to give her more.

Rising from the bed, I reach for my pants and remove my wallet, taking the condom out of the hidden pocket. Holding it between my teeth, I shove down my underwear, tear the package open and roll the condom in place.

Hovering above her on the mattress, I hold her gaze. Neither of us moves. Neither of us says a word. We stay like this a minute, letting the reality of what we are about to do settle in. Then, I press a soft kiss to her lips. I kiss her slow. I kiss her as if no one else exists.

"I love you, baby."

"I love you, too."

And then I learn about heaven.

TWENTY-SIX

CORA

Present

WHY DOES it feel like this is our first date? The passion and heat and uncertainty. Will he kiss me? Will he stay the night? What will happen once we exit the car? Should I invite him inside?

Why the hell am I so nervous? This is Gavin.

I find it funny that I feel all these things because we have done this once before. Every. Single. Part. Of course, the experience is different when you are sixteen and your hormones are on a one-way track to Sex Town. The excitement and lust are tenfold because the experience is new. But as an adult, it all just feels… different.

My heart and mind no longer ruled by my hormones. Not that I discount them because I know they lurk in the shadows. But as a woman… if Gavin and I go there. If we do this again—us—and it doesn't work out, I won't recover. Us trying to reignite what we once were, our history has been magnified times a thousand. Every memory is amplified and with more definition. Each new touch is layered with a newer meaning, a promise of forever. Something we thought we understood all those years ago, but couldn't quite grasp the magnitude.

But now... we comprehend it all. And spending forever with someone you love resonates in a whole new light.

We get out of the car and walk to the back door off of the driveway. He walks me inside and goes to the couch, Luna jumping on his lap the second he sits down. *Traitor.* But in the same breath, it melts my heart that my faithful companion has taken such an easy liking to him.

"Do you want to watch a movie?" I ask, hoping to break the pressure mounting between us. No doubt he feels it too.

"Sure. Whatever you'd like."

I kick off my shoes and settle in on the couch beside him, Luna looking at me as if I am invisible. *Double traitor.* Grabbing the remotes, I turn on the soundbar and Apple TV. After scrolling through my movie library, I click on *Hunger Games.*

Gavin wraps his arm around me and I lean into his chest, my head resting just below his shoulder. When the weight of his head rests atop mine, I sigh at the closeness we share. It has been a long time since I have had this connection. A bond that never goes away, never breaks. Something I have longed to have again, but came up empty-handed in every search.

For a brief time, I had thought maybe Jonas and I shared such a bond. But the more I tried with him, the more it felt forced and inappropriate. An imitation in a nice package. The only feelings I have for Jonas are strictly platonic. All I can hope is for his understanding. As my relationship with Gavin progresses, my relationship with Jonas will taper. Yes, I will always be his friend and he mine. But the boundary lines must be firmly drawn.

Luna purrs in Gavin's lap as the three of us cuddle on the couch. This is the closest I have felt to home in thirteen years. Warm and comfortable. As if the stars have realigned and everything is as it should be. And I pray I get to feel it every day going forward. The day Gavin left; a void took over the part of my heart reserved for him. A black hole. Life no longer functioned quite the same. The only thing that kept me going was knowing we would see each other again.

I secluded myself from friends and family. Found comfort in nothing as I sat thoughtlessly in my room, day after day. Went to school as required, but lost all sense of focus or determination. I ate less and slept more. Never left the house unless mandatory. Was forced to bathe and put on something other than pajamas or pieces of Gavin's clothes. Clothes which I refused to wash.

When minutes became hours and hours became days, days turning into weeks and months, a light inside me died. A light I thought would never burn bright again. Sure, the world wasn't quite as dim as the years became a decade and more. But now… now there is a flicker.

I wake wrapped in Gavin's arms, my body curled and pressing against his chest. Snuggling into him further, I inhale his beachy pine scent before he lays me on my bed and pulls the comforter over me. Beneath the covers, I undo my jeans, sliding them off and tossing them to the floor. He plants a kiss on my forehead and starts for the door.

"Stay." It is all I tell him. All I croak out in the darkness.

He spins around and his eyes search mine. Indecision highlights his face. So, I fold back the comforter on the other side of the bed and pat the sheet. I have no idea what the time is, but it is late and he has to be tired. No need for him to request an Uber at this late/early hour when he can just stay here.

"Are you sure?" His voice is riddled with insecurity.

"I'm tired. You're tired. We both need to sleep. So, just come lay down and get some sleep."

My words sound simple enough, but is the notion of sleeping in bed with Gavin really so simple? Sex is the furthest thing from my mind. His arms around me, though…

He hesitates a minute, watching me with an unreadable expression. Soon, his will caves and a thump hits the floor as he toes off his shoes. A second later, he tugs his shirt over his head and drops his jeans to the floor. The bed dips under his weight, the comforter shifting as he gets situated. When he stills, I roll to my side and snuggle close to him. Into him.

Oh god, how I have missed this.

For a solid minute, I swear he stops breathing. I lay my hand to the left of his sternum and feel his heart beating a vicious rhythm beneath my palm. *Is he nervous? Why on earth would he be nervous?*

"Gavin, is this okay? Me being this close," I whisper against his skin.

As his breath returns, his hand covers mine and holds it in place. His other arm snakes around my shoulders and hauls me closer. "Yes, better than okay. It's just been a long time."

I press my lips to his chest and settle against him, cocooned in his embrace. "Good night, Gavin."

"Night, baby."

My body is hot. Like I have been tanning in the sun for countless hours during mid-August slathered in tanning oil. Every inch consumed by heat and sweat. The sweltering heat inescapable and becoming far beyond unbearable. I may suffer heatstroke any second.

On the cusp of sleep and awake, I shift between the sheets and kick a leg out, hoping to cool my body. As I scoot closer to the edge, pushing the comforter down to my waist, the bed shifts beside me as a hand crawls across my belly.

In a matter of seconds, I go from foggy and semi-alert to eyes wide open and body hyper-aware.

A groan rumbles next to me, a weighted thigh draping over my waist, the calf falling down my leg. The black-out curtains in my room make it close to impossible to see anything in my room. Under normal circumstances, I would be ecstatic not to see a single thing in my room. But that doesn't apply in the current situation.

Moving as slow as humanly possible, I turn my head and look to my side. Next to me, Gavin lies asleep. His face relaxed and flaunting the soft yet masculine lines of his face. I take this quiet moment, the one where he isn't studying my every observation or movement, and absorb all the parts of him I have missed over the years.

With my eyes, I trace the thick curves of his brow. Drift down and get lost in the feather of his long, dark lashes. Follow the line and curve of his nose to the philtrum above his upper lip, the small indentation masked by a day's worth of dark stubble. Stubble I want against my soft skin. And then resting on his full pink lips.

Seconds become minutes and I can't seem to locate the strength to look away from his mouth. My own mouth waters at the sight, the temptation to lean forward and wake him with my lips pressed against his grows with every beat of my heart. But as much as I want this man—this beautiful and enigmatic man—part of me screams to keep my heart protected. Memories flash in my head like old photographs, providing me with glimpses of the past and how I crumbled when he left. How impossible it was to breathe without him here.

With every cell inside my body, I want to believe what he tells me. That he is moving back. That he has never stopped thinking of me or us or the future we always wanted. And that his only desire is to be with me again. Believing those words, those sentiments, is all I have longed for with him. All I need. I want to breathe again.

But listening to your heart and protecting it don't always go hand in hand. They are two different plates on the scale and weighed separately. And I need to make a choice on which matters most. Giving in to what my heart desires or shielding my heart from future pain.

"Good morning, baby," Gavin rasps, my body jumping at the sound.

My eyes bolt to his as if I have been caught doing something forbidden. The top length of his dark hair sits partially on the pillow and his forehead. I gaze into his steely-gray eyes, the irises a thin outline of his dilated pupils—which are immersed in me. His fixation on me is possessive and powerful. And as captivated as I am, I am also fearful and nervous.

What if we do this and we find out we are not who we used to be?

What if the affection is one-sided? Or too lopsided to make things work?

What if he moves back and it negatively impacts his career—or both of ours—and he resents me? Can we continue a happy and healthy relationship in that instance?

What if we get back together and everything is perfect?

I allow the last question to tumble through my thought processes for a moment. Allow myself to believe that us coming back together is nothing short of amazing and perfect. Allow myself to believe this is our chance at a happily ever after. One can only hope we are fortunate enough for life to ebb and flow with ease and bliss.

"I can practically hear the cogs in your head cranking. What could require so much thought this early in the morning?" Gavin's eyes bore into mine, a lighthearted act meant to bring my thoughts to life.

"It is early." Closing the gap between us, I give him a chaste kiss before continuing. "And way too early for in-depth conversations. Maybe after we have some coffee and breakfast."

His fingertips trail along my cheekbone, tracing to my ear and leaving a current in its wake as he tucks my hair behind my ear. "Breakfast sounds fantastic. Here or out?"

"I think I have everything needed here, so let's stay in. Plus, I think Luna is upset with me and the lack of attention I've been giving her over the last week. She needs a little mom time and affection."

Gavin groans as he closes his eyes, his arm drawing me in closer to his warm body. He caresses the tip of his nose over the flesh of my collarbone, skimming up the front of my throat and inhaling deep below my ear. When he speaks, his words reverberate from his chest to mine and dampen my panties.

"Mmm, I can understand the need for time and affection. If I purr and rub on your leg, will I get something in exchange?"

My breath hitches as intensity and hunger bloom between my legs. As much as I want to play-shove him, I ache to bring him impossibly closer. To tear off the remaining clothes on our bodies and rememorize every freckle and scar and curvature that has changed over the years.

But I am not ready for us to take that step yet. At least that is what I keep telling myself. Maybe if I repeat it enough times, I will believe it.

"You know you're making it really difficult to leave this bed," I whine.

"Maybe we can have a different form of breakfast," he coaxes.

"As tempting as that is, I'm going to vote we do the real food thing. I'm not sure I'm ready…" I trail off.

His thumb brushes over my cheek, eyes sweet and conveying his agreement. "Baby, I will wait forever for you. It feels as if I already have. When you're ready" — he kisses me tenderly— "that's when I'll be ready."

Although I am not ready to voice the words aloud again, all I can think about is how much I love this man. How I have always loved him, even when I had found a way to shove every memory of him and us into some desolate corner of my mind. He is my foundation, cracked or whole.

"Thank you." The words barely audible.

"For you—" he says. "Anything."

And without a care in the world, our lips and tongues do a dance as old as time.

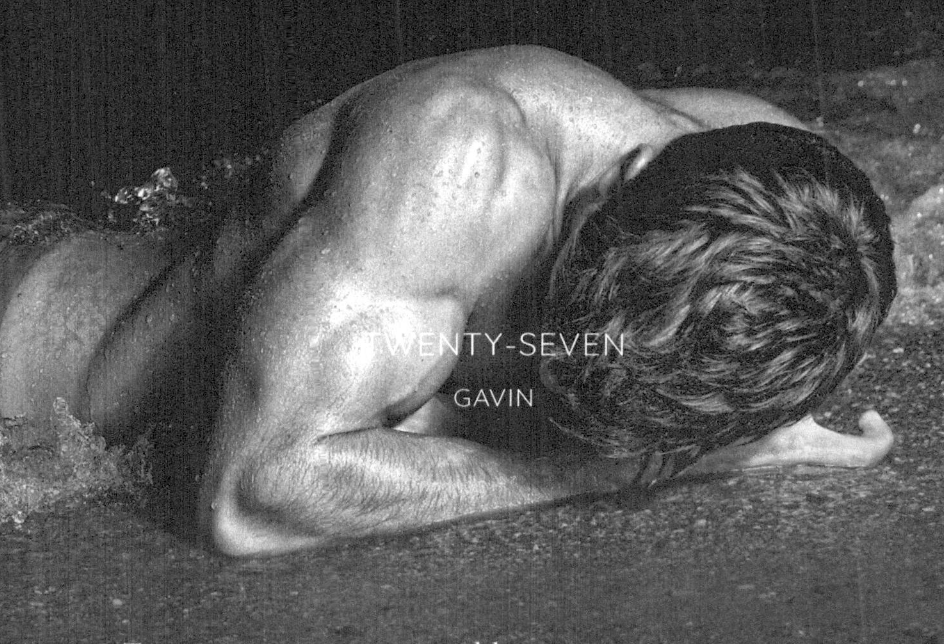

This view will never get old.

After a half hour of lips sucking and tongues tasting and hands groping, we finally decided it was best for us to get out of the bed. Not that a bed is required for the many things I want to do with her. Although we have already had sex, that time of our lives was different. Back then, everything was awkward and new and questionable.

But now…

Our time apart is not something I relish, but it does give both of us a different vantage point. For me, I respect people and life on a whole new level. Everything has a fresher perspective, is more eye-opening. That is not to say I don't do stupid shit from time to time—because don't we all. Just that I now know, understand,

and am willing to deal with the consequences of my actions. Whatever they may be.

Right now, I refuse to disguise my ogling of Cora's body. She moves around the kitchen—her back facing me—in a black cotton ribbed tank top. The hem clings to her hips while the bust line accentuates the curvature of her tits and shows a hint of natural cleavage. I know she isn't wearing a bra beneath the tank as evidenced by the occasional visual of her firm nipples against the fabric. Below the tank, cherry red low-cut boy short panties cover most of her round ass cheeks.

Watching her—I groan internally—has my dick hardening and my mouth watering. Her body is not the only part of her I love, but it is a nice bonus. The last time I got such an intimate view of her body, we were teenagers and our bodies still had a year or two of developing to go. Cora's body is as curvaceous now as it was then, but not quite the same. She has taken care of herself—diet, exercise, enjoying life as best she can—and it shows.

Cora moves around the kitchen—slicing strawberries and apples, adding them to a bowl with blueberries and squeezing a lemon over top. Stirring a large frying pan loaded with shredded potatoes, chopped onions, oil, herbs and spices. Flipping a few "sausage" links—I learned this morning Cora is slowly eliminating meat from her diet. And occasionally checking the time on her Instant Pot, where she cooks a batch of cinnamon steel-cut oatmeal.

When she told me she was removing meat from her diet, I rattled off twenty questions asking why. I also questioned whether or not the food she was making would be any good. But the savory aroma of garlic and the sweetness of maple and cinnamon flitting through the air has me hungrier than ever. The true test will be when I taste it all. Honestly, the links are the only thing I am questioning. Everything else is somewhat normal.

The Instant Pot signals it is done cooking the oatmeal as she flips the potatoes one last time. One thing I remember from our breakfast excursions years ago, Cora likes her hash browns dark with a crispy crust and tends to pile them high on her plate. And it looks as if nothing has changed in that department.

She heads to the cabinet holding the dishware, grabbing two plates and mugs. Setting the plates beside the stovetop, she pops a K-Cup in the Keurig and presses the large brew button after her mug is under the drip. When it finishes, she repeats the process for me.

Everything about this blip in time is perfect. This is how my life should be. Our life. We ebb and flow in synchronization. Natural. Comfortable. Synergistically.

As much as I tried, I never found another person who made me feel more myself than Cora. Being with her... everything just fits in place. Nothing is forced. It just... is.

"Would you like anything in your coffee? Sugar?

Creamer?" she asks, breaking me from my endless one-sided staring contest.

"Creamer. Dare I ask what my options are?" I give her my best goofy-scary face.

"I only have one and it's coconut milk-based. It's good. You'll like it," she states with confidence.

I nod. "Then that's what I'll have," I tease.

Cora adds creamer to both cups and a small spoonful of sugar to hers. She sets my cup in front of me, then turns back to the stove and begins plating the food. Before I can offer to help, she sets a plate and bowl in front of me. Within seconds, she adds maple syrup, a jar of cinnamon and a jar of garlic between our place settings. A smile perks up the corners of my mouth at the sight.

My love for maple and cinnamon.

Her indescribable love and obsession for garlic.

When we were younger, Waffle House was a regular occurrence—as it is with most teens and partiers. But she always ordered a triple portion of hash browns—scattered and smothered—and brought her own container of garlic powder. The small jar an additional accessory in her purse. I had gotten used to seeing it for the almost two years we were together. It was second nature. But seeing it today has me laughing at the fact she still has the habit.

"What are you laughing at?"

Rather than saying it, I simply point to the jar before spearing a sliced strawberry with my fork.

"There is no shame in loving garlic. If I knew you loved it, I would have added it to the hash browns. Normally, when I make my own, I add at least three or four cloves of garlic. The more, the merrier."

Shock registers in my expression. "Three or four? In a single serving? That's a lot of damn garlic, baby. You worried about vampire attacks?" I joke.

"Ha-ha," she deadpans. "No, goofball. With anything else, you build a tolerance level over time. What would be a potent level of garlic to some, I barely taste. What can I say—it's not just my favorite food, but it is also good for you." She shrugs off her response as if it should be public knowledge.

"Next time, just add the garlic in with the potatoes. I'm a big boy. I can handle it."

"Alright, big shot. As long as you promise not to bitch about it," she prompts me.

I hold up my right hand. "I swear I won't complain —" I hesitate, but continue. "Much."

She sticks her tongue out at me, crossing her eyes and cocking her head to the side. And I fall a little harder.

We spend the work-free day driving all over. She takes me to downtown St. Petersburg, where we stroll along Beach Drive, check out some of the storefronts and visit the Dali Museum. So much of downtown has changed and it is as if I am in a whole new version of an old city.

The St. Petersburg Pier is no longer there. Cora tells me it was torn down about five or six years ago. Now, a large outdoor area has taken its place. A restaurant sits closer inland and the pier is more outdoor activity focused. It is kind of weird to wander around here and not see the old inverted pyramid building. I had so much fun there as a kid. Hopefully the city builds something that adds more flare to the current structure, which seems blah in comparison.

The Dali has also been relocated and looks nothing like the original. Now it resembles a piece of art and is amazing without even stepping foot inside. But we do walk through the exhibit. Dali's work has always fascinated me, with all the droopy clocks and ants or distorted images of his wife. One of my favorites is the *Geopoliticus Child.* It just reaches me on some strange level; intrigues me.

When we leave the Dali, we opt to leave Cora's car in the garage we parked in earlier. Hand in hand, we stroll along the waterfront near the marina and eventually walk toward the shops and restaurants. After about ten minutes, we are trekking down First Avenue North.

As we head for the entrance of a restaurant to grab lunch, I push out a quiet laugh at her choice of location. No matter how much time has passed, some things about her will always be predictable. And I love that those parts of her remain. That time hasn't changed her completely. She is still the same girl I fell in love with. Only now, she is one-hundred-percent woman.

"Are you laughing at me?" she insinuates.

I squeeze her fingers with mine. "You're joking, right? I mean, I should have guessed we'd be having Asian for lunch," I tease.

"Why mess with a good thing." It is all she says, her shoulders shrugging as if eating what you love should be a given. I suppose she is right.

The hostess seats us at a table, handing us menus and letting us know our server will be with us soon. As my eyes dance over the options—sushi and non-sushi alike —I am a bit overwhelmed at the options available.

"Do you know what you're getting?" I ask Cora, praying her order will guide me in some direction.

She taps a finger to her lip. "We're about to see what you really think about me," she states, her words cryptic and confusing the hell out of me.

"Huh?"

Laughter bursts from her lips, dying quickly before she rambles off her intended order. "Here we go... I'm getting an order of spring rolls, seaweed salad, the vegetable ramen—which comes with a salad—and a yam yam sushi roll minus the eel sauce."

My gaze locks in place, the sight of her blurring. *Is she going to actually eat all of that?*

"Um. Is there something you're not telling me? That's a lot of food for just one person."

Cora just shakes her head at me. "Nope. I like ordering a lot so I have leftovers to take home. I won't eat it all while we're here. Swear," she states with a giggle.

Thank fuck. I was seriously worried some other reason had her ordering enough food for two.

"Maybe I won't need to order anything if you're getting so much," I taunt.

"Makes no difference to me. But you should get whatever you want to eat." Then she smiles and I forget what to do. I snap out of my Cora-fog and shake my head, internally laughing at myself and how easily she sidetracks me.

I scan the menu one last time as the server approaches. Gesturing for her to order first, she prattles off her mile-long lunch order. When the server looks to me, I feel like a pussy for only ordering a shrimp tempura appetizer and a Tampa roll. As if we reversed roles in the food consumption department and my masculinity has been knocked down a couple notches.

We chat while we wait for our food. And once everything is spread out on the table before us, to say I am overwhelmed would be an understatement. Everything has its own dish and there are currently seven dishes on our tiny two-person table. Seven. But I'm intrigued to see how much she actually does eat.

Bite after bite, the food begins to vanish. Needless to say, I am done eating before Cora, and all I can do is sit back and enjoy the entertainment before me. She pops a piece of her sushi in her mouth, moaning around the tempura fried sweet potato and rice. The sound stirs me up. Has me dying to hear that moan—and all other delicious sounds—with me hovering above her.

When we were younger, we'd had sex a number of times before my mother shipped us off to California. In the beginning, things were awkward and uncoordinated —as it is for anyone having sex for the first time. But the six months that followed our first time, we learned and explored many things with each other. One thing I never remember Cora doing was groaning in pleasure. It's not that she didn't enjoy sex or that she wasn't orgasming— she was just a quiet lover.

And so many parts of me want to know if that little fact still holds true.

TODAY HAS BEEN one of the best days I have experienced in a long time.

Gavin and I walked around downtown St. Petersburg for hours and had a great lunch, although he teased me endlessly about the amount of food I ordered and ate. What can I say? I love my Asian food and I love it more when I can enjoy it a second go-around.

After eating lunch, we strolled a few blocks before turning around and heading back to the parking garage. We blared music from my Spotify playlist through the speakers and drove with the windows down, the wind whipping our hair everywhere on the short stretch of interstate and highway driving. Close to an hour later, I drove over the backed up Memorial Causeway and on to popular Clearwater Beach.

As I pulled into the parking lot, Gavin spoke up for the first time since we had gotten in the car. "Come up with me."

Once I found a place to park, I looked over at Gavin, unsure of what to say.

"Come up with me," he repeats, soft-spoken.

Should I? Everything about us is molding back into place. Him asking me to come up to his room could be completely innocent. After all, he did say he would wait until I was ready before we took things further. And I believe him.

"Okay," I stammer. "Yes, I'll come up."

We hold hands from the parking lot to the bank of elevators, my bag of leftovers in his other hand. No words or sentiments are exchanged, not that they need to be. His body language and expressions tell me everything I need to know.

How much he cares for me.

How excited he is for us to be together again.

How nervous he is, his palm clammy against mine.

But most of all, how much he loves me.

Neither of us has broached the infamous *L* word, but it is there, dangling in front of us both. A few times I have almost let it slip from my lips. But I caught myself and battened down the hatches.

It's not that I don't want to tell him I love him. The complete opposite, actually. But if I allow myself to say the word, to convey the enormous level of emotion that partners up with confessing such a sentiment, it may change everything. And right now, I have no idea if the change would be for the better or worse. The way he has been around me—calling me *baby* like he did years ago—leads me to believe it would be the former.

And if I muster up the courage to profess my love for him—again—will he do the same? I can't put my heart on the line, not if I am unsure he will do the same. Not enough time has passed since his return. Not enough to know whether or not he will run off again.

The elevator pings when we reach his floor and we step out. Retrieving his wallet from his back pocket, he unlocks the door and ushers me in. With a loud thump, the door closes and he wanders over to the kitchenette, placing my food in the refrigerator. I stand in the entryway, staring at the room and how messy it looks. It is obvious he has told the maid service to ignore his room, which makes me want to laugh.

Thirty minutes later, we sit cuddled on a small loveseat, laughing at an episode of *Lucifer* on Netflix. We munch on chips and candy he had purchased on his first night here. The episode is almost over when a knock sounds at the door.

We both look at each other, confused. Before we started watching the show, we talked about grabbing dinner after, but not from room service. Maybe the maid was upset over not being able to clean his room for more than a week.

Gavin rises from the couch, kissing me on the crown of my head. "Probably someone knocking on the wrong door. I'll be back in a sec."

His bare feet pad across the floor as he disappears from my direct line of sight. The loud clunk of the deadbolt disengaging echoes in the room, followed by a slight creak of hinges. When he got up to leave the couch, he had paused the show and created a vacant silence in the room. Right now, that silence is deafening.

Mumbled voices come from where Gavin went to open the door. A door which has yet to be closed. Which means whoever is at the door is either lost or is someone Gavin knows. My stomach suddenly constricts, a heavy sickness settling in my core.

Is it Alyson? Is she giving him more shit regarding us?

Curious as to what is taking Gavin so long to return, I rise from the couch and walk toward the door, my stride quiet and slow. The closer I get, the clearer I hear the conversation. A woman's voice chirps from the hall, her words sweet and her tone casual. And I determine by their exchange she is someone Gavin knows. And knows well. And it isn't Alyson.

When I take a few more steps, I hear Gavin muttering under his breath, anger seeping into his voice. A couple more steps and I can see the door. Can see Gavin's back and the slightest bit of wavy, blonde locks. His words to her are venomous as he tries to make her leave. But when he shifts to his left an inch or so, she catches sight of me and a devilish smile takes over her features.

Who the hell is this woman?

Thirteen years ago

"What do you mean you're moving?" I ask, tears welling in my eyes and threatening to spill at any second.

He runs his fingers through his hair, grabbing hold at the roots and yanking as he bows his head. "My mom. She got transferred; promoted. Whatever. But her new position is in California. So, we have to move." He tugs his hair harder before releasing it from his grip and looking at me with bloodshot eyes.

I have no clue what to say. Or what to do. How to react. In this situation, is there really anything I can do? There is no way I can stop his mom from accepting the promotion she rightfully deserves. Nor can I stop her from taking the only person I care about to the other side of the country, almost three thousand miles away. If we were older, maybe we would have a say.

Covering my face with my hands, I mumble, "When?" Although, I am terrified to know the answer.

"She said we're leaving next week," he says, his voice cracking at the end.

"Next week?" I whisper. "But what about school? And us?" My voice shrinking the more I speak.

A vignette darkens the edges of my vision. My world slowly closing in on itself. Nausea roils in my belly and crawls up my throat.

He wraps his arms around me, enveloping me in a tight embrace. His warmth is pure comfort, and I close my eyes and allow myself a moment to get lost in the feel of him. Breathe in his scent, the earthy beach smell that only Gavin has. Hear the sound of his erratic heartbeat beneath my ear on his chest. My head shifting with the rise and fall of his lungs.

He can't leave. He just can't. Gavin is home. Where I belong. And I am where he belongs.

One of his hands caresses the back of my head as his lips pepper small kisses on the crown while he shushes me. Our bodies rock back and forth, the movement subtle. And I squeeze him as tight as humanly possible, my body trembling as I am wracked with sobs. Maybe if I hold him tight enough, he won't leave.

"We'll figure something out, baby. This is just as painful for me as it is you. I don't want to leave," he confesses. "Not you. Not here. You are my home, Cora." He echoes my internal sentiment.

"You're my home, too," I reply as tears flood my cheeks. "If you're not here, I'll be so lost."

He wraps me more securely in his arms as if he is trying to prevent the eventual departure we both know we have no control over. I wish it were that simple. I wish we had a say in the matter. A voice. But we don't and that hurts even more.

He withdraws from me, bringing his fingers to my chin and tipping my head back. Our tear-stained, puffy red eyes hold each other's. The pain in my chest swells more with each passing second. My lungs burn as I refuse to breathe in this form of reality. This cannot be happening. This cannot be real. If I don't believe it, maybe it won't happen. Maybe he won't leave.

"I will find a way back to you, baby. It may not be right away. But never doubt that I will return. The only place I want to be is beside you. Forever."

A heavy sigh escapes my lips. *Why could this have not waited another two years? When he could stay behind.*

"I love you, Gavin," I tell him, and it reaches deeper than the hundreds of times I have told him before.

He brushes a cluster of stray hairs from my face, tucking them behind my ear. "And I love you, Cora. More than anything else in existence."

I sniffle back my tears and congested nasal phlegm, the sound and motion very unladylike. We both laugh at me. But when we stop, both our faces locked in serious expressions, I whisper-rasp, "Happy Birthday, Gavin."

And seconds later he has me wrapped in his arms again.

I help Gavin put the last of his things in a cardboard box, closing the flaps and sealing it with tape. Grabbing the Sharpie on the floor, I write *Gavin's room* on the box and proceed to doodle a quick image of a beach beside it. If having a small drawing by my hand on cardboard is the only piece of me he can take with him, I will draw on every box possible.

"Thanks," he mutters, his mood growing infinitely more sour as we packed up his life here. I don't blame him. If our roles were reversed, I would behave the same.

"You're welcome."

Looking around his room, I take in the bare blue walls. Before he was required to pack everything he owned, the walls had been littered with rock band posters and concert flyers. Images of surfers and the beach and us as well as our friends. Now, all those pieces rest in boxes or tubes, waiting to be added to new walls. In a new house. Thousands of miles from here.

The built-in bookshelf is now coated in a layer of dust after his collection of magazines and books got tucked away and packed inside the large moving truck outside. All the furniture had been taken out of his room a few hours ago. The carpet depressed from the feet of the bed and dresser, and outlined with the faded color where the sunlight couldn't reach.

His room now a skeleton of a space I once deemed comforting and warm. His room as hollow as the hole growing in my chest.

He lifts the box from the floor and heads for the door. The last box. And the last time we would be in his room. I carry the packing tape and marker, trudging down the hall and blindly following his footsteps.

With each step we take, the world as I know it slips further and further away. No more lunches at school or meetups before or after. No more laughter or teasing. And no more movie nights or walks on the beach or sunsets. Or holding hands, embraces, or lips against mine. No more Gavin. And no more us.

By the time we reach the moving truck, tears flow like rivers down my cheeks. I do my best to make no sounds, but the restraint it requires is fading fast. It feels as if I am intentionally giving the love of my life away. Shoving everything he owns into this truck and saying goodbye forever. Packing him up and shipping him off to who knows where.

Over the last week, we spent every possible moment together. Not a moment wasted. Yes, he had to pack up his life. But he tried to do that after curfew so we could have as much us time as possible. Yet it feels as if we had no time at all. It feels as if every moment we have shared for the last two years is being ripped away and shredded into a million pieces.

As soon as he gets to California, I bet I won't hear from him often. He will be busy unpacking and adjusting to a new school just before the year ends. It isn't only a major adjustment for me, but more so for him. Not only is he losing me—losing us—he is also being thrown into a foreign place with zero friends. The only people there to comfort him are his parents. The people upending his life.

He sets the box in the truck, taking the tape and marker from my hands and placing them beside it.

Before I can think of a single word to say, he yanks me close and holds me as if his life depends on it. On me. My sobs come faster and harder. His chest shakes around me with his own turmoil. Anguish and heartache leak from both of us and there isn't a damn thing we can do about it.

Minutes later, his dad taps on his shoulder and tells him it is time for them to leave.

After a few labored breaths, he pulls back with hesitancy. His eyes swollen and red as he looks into mine. "I love you, baby. Hopefully, I can come back during the summer." He kisses me and steals my breath, my pulse soaring in my veins.

"I love you, too, Gavin. Call me when you land."

We exchange one last kiss and embrace, and then he is whisked away. My legs giving out as I collapse to the ground, where I cry for the next three hours. Alone. In the front yard of the boy I love. The boy who just left.

THIRTY

GAVIN

Present

WHEN I OPEN THE DOOR, I am beyond shocked to see Layla in the hall.

"Hey," she singsongs, waving a hand at me.

"What are you *doing* here?" I whisper-yell. "And how did you know where my room is?"

Her bright smile fades as her brows furrow in confusion. "I had a shoot in Miami. Just thought I'd surprise you on my way home. Alyson adjusted my flight for me, so I'm here till tomorrow morning. She told me which room you were in and suggested you might want to grab dinner."

What. The. Actual. Fuck. Alyson?

She knows Cora and I have been working on mending our relationship. And she also knows I have every intention of moving back to Florida as soon as I can sort out the details. Is this her play on keeping me in California? Sending Layla to my door and having her attempt to swoon me over dinner.

Not that Layla could ever hold my attention in that way.

Now I have got some choice words for Alyson the next time we talk. And they won't be pleasant. In fact, they will be downright ugly.

"That was nice of her, but I already have plans for the evening," I tell her as I start closing the door.

Her hand comes up, preventing the door from moving any farther into the frame. "What the hell, Gavin? So, *you have plans* and now I'm no longer good enough to be around?"

I really wish she would lower her fucking voice. Not only do I not want Cora hearing her, but I also don't need the people staying in the other rooms to hear her flipping her shit. I give her a pointed look, telling her to quiet down. She huffs and rolls her eyes like she gives two shits what anyone else thinks. After all, Layla is quite the attention whore.

"It's not that. I have plans with someone else. Plain and simple. Please don't try to peg me as the bad guy here. If you would've called or texted me and told me you were coming, I could have made different plans," I press, my body heating and becoming more anxious with each passing second I am away from Cora. As it is, I have been at the door far too long for it to be a wrong room situation.

"Why are you being such a dick?"

"Me? You randomly show up and expect me to drop whatever it is I am doing because you're here. Sorry. Doesn't work that way."

She needs to fucking leave. Now.

"You're different," she accuses. "Alyson was right."

"What the fuck does *that* mean?" Now Alyson is talking shit behind my back. I groan as I picture Alyson calling Layla in for interference. And at this point, pissed doesn't even begin to cover how I feel.

"Don't worry, she didn't go into any specific details with me. But she told me you've changed since being out here. That you plan to make bigger changes, too."

Tomorrow, Alyson and I are going to sit down and have a very detailed conversation about keeping her mouth shut and her nose out of other people's business. One—I pay her. Two—her job is to do what's best for me, not her. And in no way is this benefiting me. This is all about her. I cannot believe she brought Layla here, purposely changed her flight and gave her my room number. What sort of game does she think she is playing? Does she seriously think this will sway my decision? My privacy is more invaded than ever now and a newfound rage builds inside me. A rage neither Alyson nor Layla will enjoy.

"Not that it is any of your business, but yes. I plan on

moving back to Florida after I get a few things situated in California."

"You cannot be serious. How will you work from here? What is so goddamn alluring about this place?"

I shift my weight, her questions irritating me. This conversation is done. And I'm done. With her and Alyson.

Just as I am about to shut the door again, a wicked grin lights up Layla's face. A grin I know all too well. One that tells me she is about to do something spiteful and vindictive. Her eyes look past me, over my shoulder and into the room.

The hair on the back of my neck stands at attention. A boulder sinks in my gut. Before I even turn around, I know Cora is standing behind me. I *feel* her. More than likely, she was curious as to what was taking me so long to return. She has no idea who Layla is, but Layla knows about her. Not her name, but that the one person I cared about most lives here. Right now, I am one-hundred-percent certain she knows this is her. And I know her well enough to know she is about to fuck everything up.

Before I turn to face Cora, I give Layla a glare of warning. Wordlessly telling her to keep her mouth shut and leave. But her smile grows wider and I know nothing good will come of this.

"Gavin—" Cora calls out behind me. "Is everything okay?"

I school my expression and turn to face her. "Everything is fine." I want to add more, but I am at a loss for what to say.

"Hi," Layla speaks up, my body going rigid at the sound. "I'm Layla. And you are?"

Layla extends her hand in Cora's direction, but I step in front of her and block their possible connection. I don't want her touching Cora, let alone getting within arm's length.

"And you need to leave," I tell her over my shoulder, trying once more to close the door.

"Why are you being so rude, Gavin?" Layla says, her pitch an octave higher and she reaches out and touches my bicep. I cringe away from her and start pushing the door closed, only to be met with Layla's boot.

"Gavin, what's going on?" Cora asks, hundreds of questions skittering across her face.

"Yeah, Gavin, what's going on?" Layla's tone becomes venomous and shrill.

I stand between the two of them, hoping this nightmare will end. Praying I fell asleep while Cora and I were watching television and this is all one huge, fucked-up dream. But somewhere in the back of my mind, I know it isn't. And Layla is really standing here. And I am about to lose Cora all over again. Because what other plausible reason would Alyson have for bringing Layla here? None. Not a single one. And I don't know which emotion holds more power over me in this moment—fear or fury.

The silence in the room has every nerve in my body on edge. My heart slams against my ribcage, grabbing the bones and rattling like a madman. I can't breathe. Can't speak. The light at the end of a very long tunnel slowly dims and fades. I have no idea what to do. Where to be. How to function. But just as I am about to spew out something, Layla shatters the silence in the room. Along with everything that matters in my life.

"Well, since no one else is speaking, I guess I'll take the stage." Layla steps closer to me, her hands clasping around my arm. "Like I said, I'm Layla. Gavin's fiancée."

Fuuuuck…

Continue Gavin & Cora's story in Time Exposure!

Thirteen years ago, I abandoned the love of my life.
Thirteen years ago, the love of my life vanished without a word.

Fate has given us another chance.
Jealousy is trying to rip us apart.

I refuse to lose her again.
Will he actually come back to me?

Cora said words mean nothing. Not unless I back them with actions. I will flip my world upside down. Relinquish everything. All for her.

Gavin said he will fix everything. Fix us. His promises are unreliable. Until I see it with my own eyes, hope is not an option. My heart can't handle it.

Fate brought us back together, but time and distance change people.
Can we overcome our obstacles? Will our love stand the test of time?

Thank You!

Thank you so much for reading **Through the Lens**, book one in the **Click Duet**. If you would take a moment to leave a review on the retailer site where you made your purchase, Goodreads and/or BookBub, it would mean the world to me.

Reviews help other readers find and enjoy the book as well.

Much love,
    Persephone

Click Duet Playlist

Here are some of the songs from the *Click Duet* playlist. You can listen to the entire playlist on Spotify!

I Still Wait For You - XYLØ
Malibu Nights - LANY
i love you - Billie Eilish
High School Sweethearts - Melanie Martinez
The Beach - The Neighbourhood
Falling - Harry Styles
Out Of Love - Alessia Cara
BLUE - Troye Sivan, Alex Hope

The Inked Duet

A man with a broken heart and a woman scared to put herself out there. Love is never easy. Sometimes love rips you apart. Fine Line (Inked Duet #1) and Love Buzz (Inked Duet #2) is a second chance at love, single parent romance with a pinch of angst and dash of suspense.

The Insomniac Duet

He was her high school bully. She was the outcast that secretly crushed on him. More than ten years later, he's her boss, completely oblivious to their shared past, and wants no one but her. More importantly, he doesn't understand her animosity toward him.

Transcendental

A musician in search of his muse and a woman grieving the loss of her husband. Two weeks at an exclusive retreat and their connection rivals all others. Until she leaves early without notice. But he refuses to give up until he finds her again.

Depths Awakened

A small town romance which captivates you from the

start. Two broken souls have sworn off love. Vowed to never lose anyone else. But their undeniable attraction brings them together and refuses to let go.

Distorted Devotion
Swept off her feet by love, life takes a dark, unexpected turn. Now the love of her life may be the cause of her death. Check out this gripping, romantic suspense.

Ink Veins
Persephone Autumn's debut collection, Ink Veins, explores topics of depression, love, and self-discovery with a raw, unfiltered voice.

Broken Metronome
When the music of the heart dies...
Broken Metronome is an angsty poetry collection full of heartache and the possibility of what may have been.

Connect with Persephone

Connect with Persephone

www.persephoneautumn.com

Subscribe to Persephone's Newsletter

www.persephoneautumn.com/newsletter

Join Persephone's Reader Group

Persephone's Playground

Follow Persephone Online

instagram.com/persephoneautumn

facebook.com/persephoneautumnwrites

goodreads.com/persephoneautumn

bookbub.com/authors/persephone-autumn

amazon.com/author/persephoneautumn

pinterest.com/persephoneautumn

twitter.com/PersephoneAutum

Acknowledgments

Always at the top of my list… my family.

To my wife for dealing with my rambling, wacky schedule and need to pull my hair out on occasion. No matter what happens, you let me get it out before I go homicidal. And you're the best pimp. Love you!

To my daughter for always being my cheerleader and helping me navigate the ever changing world of social media. I can't wait until to pay you to do it all. Love you!

To my dad, who graciously takes my books and supports every adventure I take. Love you!

To Ellie and Rosa at My Brother's Editor… you ladies are a dynamic duo. Cleaning up my manuscripts, providing insight, and saying all the best things. Love you!

To Kat Savage… I love your face! Thank you for always making my books beautiful. And thank you for your wisdom and expertise when I ask or suggest really stupid shit. That's why I don't do graphic design.

To all the party people in Persephone's Playground… my level of gratitude for your continuous support puts a smile on my face. Thank you for always being there, for reading my words and getting excited for more. Love you!

To my ARC and promo team… being an author is hard! You help make it easier. Thank you for helping me spread the word, reading my books and giving your input and feedback. I am forever grateful for all you do!

To all my author peeps… thank you times a thousand! We all understand the insanity of being an author and I'm so lucky to have so many wonderful people in my corner. Dee Lagasee, Kat Savage, Mel Walker, Andi Burns, Ellie Isaacson, Elle Thorpe, Victoria Ellis, Christina Hart, J.R. Rogue, JA Stone, TK Cherry, Carmel Rhodes, QB Tyler, Harlow Layne and a super long list that grows longer each day. I love each and every one of you!

To Shelly… no matter what, you support everything I do! I wish there were GIFs that would reach through the screen and hug people. I'd hug you daily for all the love and support you give. Thank you for every shared post and kind word! xoxo

To every person who purchased this book… thank you so much for reading my words. Not a single day goes by where I am not humbled by people enjoying the stories I put on paper. No set of words will express my never-ending gratitude. Thank you on repeat! xoxo

About the Author

Persephone Autumn lives in Florida with her wife, crazy dog, and two lover-boy cats. A proud mom with a cuckoo grandpup. An ethnic food enthusiast who has fun discovering ways to veganize her favorite non-vegan foods. If given the opportunity, she would intentionally get lost in nature.

For years, Persephone did some form of writing; mostly journaling or poetry. After pairing her poetry with images and posting them online, she began the journey of writing her first novel.

She mainly writes romance, but on occasion dips her toes in other works. Look for her poetry publications and a psychological horror under P. Autumn.